Deadly

Circumstances

A MARY O'REILLY PARANORMAL MYSTERY

(Book Sixteen)

by

Terri Reid

DEADLY CIRCUMSTANCES – A MARY
O'REILLY PARANORMAL MYSTERY

by

Terri Reid

Copyright © 2015 by Terri Reid

All rights reserved. Without limiting the
rights under copyright reserved above, no part of this
publication may be reproduced, stored in or
introduced into a retrieval system, or transmitted, in
any form, or by any means (electronic, mechanical,
photocopying, recording, or otherwise) without the
prior written permission of both the copyright owner
and the above publisher of this book.

This is a work of fiction. Names, characters,
places, brands, media, and incidents are either the
product of the author's imagination or are used
fictitiously. The author acknowledges the
trademarked status and trademark owners of various
products referenced in this work of fiction, which
have been used without permission. The publication/
use of these trademarks is not authorized, associated
with, or sponsored by the trademark owners.

ii

The author would like to thank all those who have contributed to the creation of this book: Richard Reid, Sarah Powers and Hillary Gadd. Also, thank you to the wonderful folks at the Joiner History Room, DeKalb County Archives, Sycamore, Illinois and Sue Breese, their director, for not only helping with the research for this book, but also allowing me to feature Fred in the story. Of course, this book would not have been nearly as much fun without Margo Taylor letting me bring her along for the ride. So, thanks to Margo and my dear friend, Ann Charles, another one of those odd mystery writers.

She would also like to thank all of the wonderful readers who walk with her through Mary and Bradley's adventures and encourage her along the way. I hope we continue on this wonderful journey for a long time.

Prologue

The two-lane highway snaked through the rolling hills, farmland and woods of Northwest Illinois. The sun was low in the sky, setting the autumn colors in the trees ablaze with light. It had been a perfect Indian summer day, bright blue sky, temperatures in the high sixties and a refreshing breeze in the air. But the day was ending, and as red-tailed hawks drifted high in the sky above their car, Shirley Koch broke the uncomfortable silence that had been their passenger for nearly twenty minutes.

"We need to talk about it," she said, sitting in the passenger seat of their black sedan as they drove along the winding roads that led to the small tourist town of Galena, Illinois.

"I don't want to talk about it," Frasier Koch, her husband, stated firmly, keeping his eyes on the twisting and hilly highway.

"Well, whether you want to or not, we've got to," Shirley argued. "It's out there now and it's got to be addressed."

He glanced quickly in her direction and tightened his lips. Even though they'd been married for over fifty years, she still didn't understand him.

"Oh, I understand you all right," Shirley said, surprising him by reading his thoughts. "I'm just not

1

going to let you get away with it this time. He hurt your feelings."

With a soft sigh, Frasier shook his head. "What you don't understand is that men don't have to get in touch with their feelings," he explained. "We get mad, we hit something and then we get over it. I'll get over it."

Shirley snorted. "You'd like me to believe that," she replied. "But in reality, you get hurt and then you take your bad mood out on the people you love and trust."

"I would never do that," he replied quickly, but a look of disbelief was Shirley's only response. He sighed and nodded. "Okay, I might do that. Occasionally. But really, I don't need to talk about it."

"Really?" she asked skeptically. "Your own son treats you with little or no respect just because you won't loan him more money."

Frasier shrugged. "I guess he was counting on me."

"He needs to learn to count on himself," his wife replied and then her voice softened. "We both love Eddie. We both want what's best for him. But, at this point in his life, he shouldn't be relying on his parents."

"Well, it's all going to be his once we're gone," he replied.

"I don't know about you, but I've got a lot more living to do," Shirley said with a smile. "You promised to take me to Europe."

"What?" he exclaimed. "I never promised to take you to Europe. I told you we could visit your sister in Texas."

She shrugged. "What's the difference?" she asked. "You get packed, you get on a plane, you get off a plane and all around you everyone speaks with a funny accent. We might as well go to Europe."

He chuckled as he started to slow to take a turn, but the chuckle turned to a gasp when he pressed the brake and the car didn't slow.

"Hey, Mario, you took that corner pretty fast," Shirley remarked, grabbing hold of the door handle and pressing her feet against the floorboards. "You want to slow down?"

"Can't," Frasier gasped as he white-knuckled the steering wheel. "There's something wrong with the brakes."

"Can you put it in a lower gear?" she asked.

Frasier shifted the car down into second gear. He winced as he heard the transmission groan in

3

protest. But the car continued to accelerate as it rushed down the steep hill.

"We're coming to that hairpin curve," Shirley exclaimed, her breath coming out in frightened gasps. "You've got to slow the car down."

"I'm trying sweetheart," Frasier replied, sweat rolling down his face. "I'm trying."

The yellow sign warned of the turn and cautioned that the maximum speed for the curve was thirty-five miles per hour. Frasier glanced down at the speedometer, he was going over eighty. "I love you, Shirley," he whispered as he leaned into the curve.

"I love you, too, Frasier," she called back.

She reached over and put her hand on his arm just before the car broke through the guardrail and tumbled into the ditch, rolled over several times, and finally crashed upside-down into a utility pole. Except for the front tire turning drunkenly on a twisted axle, there was no other movement from the car.

Chapter One

Mary O'Reilly-Alden woke up with someone kicking her in the ribs, from the inside out. "Ouch," she whispered, rubbing her swollen stomach softly. "You need to be nicer to your mommy."

"Are you okay?" Bradley murmured, rolling over and peering over his wife's shoulder.

"Your son is abusing me," Mary replied with a soft smile. "He seems to think that my ribs were created for soccer practice."

Leaning closer and placing a kiss on her neck, Bradley shook his head. "Football practice," he said. "He's going for the extra point."

"Soccer," Mary insisted. "That way no one tackles him."

"Football," Bradley insisted. "But he can be the placekicker, so he only goes out on the field occasionally and makes lots of money."

Mary looked up at him. "He won't get tackled?" she asked, her eyebrows raised.

"The opposing team isn't supposed to tackle the kicker," Bradley said. "It's called roughing the kicker."

Mary looked down at her belly. "So, what do you think, Mikey?" she asked. She bent her head forward as if she could hear him. "Ah, well, that makes sense."

Grinning, Bradley met Mary's eyes. "And what did he say?" he asked.

Mary smiled back at him. "He said he wants to be a swimmer, like his daddy," Mary replied.

"Oh, he did, did he?" he asked, rolling Mary over towards him. "What if I ask him?"

"Be my guest," she said, lifting her pajama top to expose her belly.

Laying his head on her belly, his face turned towards Mary's, he whispered, "Mikey, it's Daddy. We have to have a serious conversation here."

Mary giggled, and her stomach moved. "Hey, no interference," he said with a smile.

"Sorry," she smiled back.

"So, Mikey, how do you feel about football?" he asked.

Suddenly Mary's stomach shifted, and Bradley felt a foot shoved against his cheek. Surprised, Bradley jumped away from Mary. "Whoa, he's got a powerful kick," he exclaimed.

"Tell me about it," Mary replied sardonically.

"Well, that pretty much settles it," Bradley said.

"Settles what?" Mary asked.

"He has to be a placekicker," Bradley replied. "With a kick like that, he'd be propelled right out of the water."

Laughing softly, Mary folded her hands over her stomach and shook her head. "I'm afraid your father is going to be disappointed, Mikey," Mary said to her unborn child.

Bradley sighed dramatically and then leaned over and kissed Mary. "That's okay, I disappointed my dad, too," he said.

Wrapping her arms around his neck, she shook her head. "I can't believe that you ever disappointed anyone, Bradley Alden," she replied. "Least of all your father."

"Well," he said with a casual shrug, "it's a long story."

She studied him for a moment. The attempt at a casual shrug was the clue. There was a lot more to this story than he was saying. "Tell me," she prompted.

Lifting his head, he sniffed the air. "It's a miracle," he whispered.

She smiled at him, playing along. "What's a miracle?"

"There is bacon cooking in my house, and neither you nor I are downstairs in the kitchen," he replied, wagging his eyebrows.

"Ma," she said with a happy smile. "Can we just keep her here?"

"Your dad might argue," Bradley supplied.

"He's so selfish," Mary replied with a grin.

Rolling off the bed, Bradley picked up both his and Mary's robe. "So, do we take the time to wash up and get dressed so we're decent?" he asked. "Or do we just throw on our robes and hurry downstairs?"

"Well, let's see," Mary said, slowly sliding out of the bed. "It's more than likely Clarissa, my parents, my brothers, Ian, Rosie and Stanley, and the entire Brennan family will be downstairs."

Bradley lifted the robe and then glanced at the bathroom door. "So?" he asked.

Grabbing the robe from him, Mary slipped it on with a smile. "So we go downstairs with our robes on before they eat all the bacon."

Chuckling, Bradley slipped on his robe. "Brilliant assessment, my dear," he laughed.

Chapter Two

"You're finally awake," Clarissa cried as Mary and Bradley came down the stairs. True to Mary's hypothesis, the entire first floor of their home was filled with their family and friends.

"I tried to get him to wake up earlier," Mary said, elbowing Bradley lightly. "But he's such a lazy head."

Placing his arm around her shoulders, he smiled. "Well, it's just because I lead such a boring life," he teased.

Margaret O'Reilly bustled forward, an apron tied around her waist. "Well, there's two seats at the end of the table ready for you," she said. "And how would you like your eggs?"

"Really, Ma," Mary began, "you don't—"

"Sit yourself down, young lady," her mother interrupted. "And tell me how you'd like those eggs."

"Scrambled, ma'am," Mary replied obediently with a smile. She leaned over and gave her mother a kiss on the cheek. "Thank you, Ma."

"And you, young man?" she asked Bradley.

He leaned over, too, and planted a kiss on her other cheek. "Sunnyside up," he said. "And I'll sit down immediately."

"Good boy," Ma replied with a grin, turning back to the stove to start their eggs.

"I wasn't brave enough to ask her about bacon," Bradley whispered to Mary.

"Auch, you don't have to worry about that," Ian said, coming up behind them. "She's been guarding the bacon like a she-bear guards her cubs. Three pieces for each person, and if there's enough leftover once everyone has eaten, then you can come back."

Mary chuckled. "That's my mom."

She sat down, and Ian slid a small paper-toweled covered plate in front of her. "What's this?" she asked.

"Appetizers," Ian said with a wink.

Uncovering the plate, she found three small slices of the cheesecakes they'd had for dessert the night before. "Oh, Ian," she breathed. "Thank you."

"Why don't I get cheesecake in the morning?" Bradley grumbled.

"Because you don't look fresh-as-a-daisy and incredibly sexy even with no makeup on at seven months pregnant," Ian replied easily.

Mary blushed slightly. "Thank you, Ian," she replied. "I don't even need the cheesecake now, I feel so good."

Bradley sighed. "Well, I'm depressed," he teased. "Ian doesn't think I look sexy."

Mary nearly spit out her first bite of cheesecake. "Ah, well, don't worry dear," she soothed. "You really aren't Ian's type."

"Eggs up," Margaret called from across the room, removing the eggs from the griddle and sliding them onto a plate already filled with bacon and toast. Before she glanced their way, Bradley deftly dropped the napkin over the cheesecakes and slid them onto the chair next to them.

"Well done," Ian whispered.

"My hero," Mary added.

"This is what you need," her mother said, putting the plates in front of them. "Good hearty food to start the day." She looked at Ian for a moment. "And then once you finish your breakfast, you can eat the treats this scallywag absconded for you."

"Yes, Ma," Mary replied, biting back a smile.

"Pardon, Mrs. O'Reilly," Ian added, feeling like a ten year-old schoolboy.

Once Margaret had walked away from the table, Mary exhaled softly. "She has eyes in the back of her head," she whispered.

"Aye, and an extra set of ears, too," Margaret called from across the room.

12

The three adults stared at each other for just a moment and then Mary and Bradley dug into their breakfast. "Where's Mike?" Mary asked Ian between bites.

"He said something about meeting with a couple that had visited your closet last night," Ian said, his look puzzled. "Did I get that right?"

Mary smiled and nodded. "Yes, at least one of them wasn't quite aware of the new rules," she said. "Did he say where he was going to meet them?"

"Your office," he replied. "He said he'd let you know anything he found out."

"How about some milk?" Bradley asked Mary.

"I'd love some," she replied.

When he stood, Ian leaned a little closer to Mary and handed her an envelope. "He also asked me to give you this," he whispered.

Mary opened it and found an invitation to Bradley's high school reunion. "It's tonight," she said softly. "I wonder why he didn't mention it to me."

"Mike figured it was either because he thought you would be too tired or he completely forgot about it," Ian said with a smile. "But Mike also thought that this was the first reunion Bradley would be able to go to without bad memories about Jeannine. He really thought you should go."

"Well then," Mary said, with a shrug. "I guess we'll go."

Chapter Three

Two hours later, their house was not only quiet but also neat and tidy. Mary was sitting on the couch, regretting the blueberry muffin she'd been tempted to eat on top of everything else that morning. "I ate too much," she moaned softly, stretching out on the couch.

"You do know that gluttony is one of the seven deadly sins," Mike said as he appeared next to the couch.

She laid her head on the back of the couch and closed her eyes. "Now I know why," she said. "I feel like I'm going to explode."

He glanced around the room slowly. "You'd really make a mess if you do," he replied. "And your mom did such a great job of tidying everything up before she left."

Mary opened her eyes. "She really did, didn't she?" Mary replied. "Ma is amazing. I had to threaten her in order to help this morning. And you can't even tell that hordes of hungry people invaded my house this morning."

Smiling, Mike nodded. "Well, except from the groans coming from you and from Bradley," he replied.

Mary grinned. "Bradley, too?" she asked. "I thought he was on the porch putting away all of the Halloween paraphernalia."

"He is," Mike said with a chuckle. "But he's not happy."

"It's not our fault," Mary said. "We were just being polite. I mean, Rosie went through all the trouble of making those delicious, giant, blueberry muffins. We really couldn't turn one down."

"No, you're right," Mike agreed with a slight touch of irony. "And you wouldn't want to be rude."

She grinned. "See, I feel so much better when you agree with me. So how did the meeting go with my closet visitors?" she asked. "Do I need to meet with them?"

Mike hovered over to the chair next to the couch and sat down. "Yes, you will," he said. "They're going to need your help. But their case can wait for a day or so. I really need you to go with Bradley to the high school reunion tonight."

Nodding, she lifted her head and propped her feet up on the ottoman. "Ian mentioned it to me this morning," she said. "Is it just for Bradley, or are other people involved?"

Mike sighed slowly. "I don't know all the answers," he said. "I just know it's complicated and Bradley needs to be there."

"Okay, I can do complicated," she replied with a shrug. "But I have one really important question about tonight."

"Yes?" Mike asked.

"Do I need a formal dress?"

Chuckling, he shook his head. "No, it's a reunion associated with the Homecoming game, so it's being held in the gym and it's casual dress."

"Excellent, I can do casual, no problem," she replied.

"Just get him there," Mike said.

"Don't worry," she said. "You can count on me."

Just then, the front door opened and Bradley walked in, fake spider webs, orange pumpkin lights and other Halloween paraphernalia tangled around his head and neck. Mike looked at Bradley and then back at Mary. "Yeah, I think I better fade out now," he said softly, fading as he spoke.

"Coward," she whispered back as she used the couch arm to push herself up.

"What happened to you?" Mary asked Bradley, walking across the room towards him.

"I think I was just assaulted by a Halloween display," he said with a little chagrin. "I thought I could get it all down at once, and then it came down, all at once."

She walked up to him and shook her head. "Turn around," she ordered, untangling the spider webs from the pumpkin lights. "I have to start from the back and work my way around."

At that moment, Clarissa came bounding down the stairs with her backpack in tow. She stopped at the bottom of the stairs, glanced at Mary quickly and then looked at Bradley. "Can I spend the night at the Brennan's? Please?" she asked.

Bradley glanced around her to the backpack on the ground. "It looks like you're already packed," he said.

Biting her lower lip, Clarissa stole a quick look at Mary.

"Well, actually," Mary inserted, "I spoke to Katie before they left and asked her about Clarissa spending the night."

Bradley turned to Mary. "Why?"

"Because then we could go to your high school reunion tonight," she replied.

He opened his mouth, then closed it and then opened it again. "How did you know about that?" he asked.

She shrugged. "Mike might have mentioned it to me," she said and bit back her laughter at his aggrieved look.

"Mary, you don't need to go to my reunion," he said. "You're too tired, and you don't get enough rest."

Clarissa cleared her throat lightly. "Even if Mommy is too tired, can I still spend the night at the Brennan's?"

Mary grinned and looked wide-eyed at Bradley. "Can she?" she asked.

"Yes," he replied. "Yes, you can. Do you need me to walk you over?"

Clarissa looked at her father, still covered with Halloween, and decidedly shook her head. "No, someone might see us," she said, grabbing her backpack and boosting it over her shoulder.

"Ouch," Bradley replied. "I think I look pretty cool."

Clarissa stared at her dad for a moment and then slowly nodded. "Sure, Dad, you look really cool," she replied. "And you should think about wearing webs all the time. It's a good look."

18

He tried to bite back a grin. "You are such a brat."

She grinned. "Besides, Maggie and Mrs. Brennan are waiting on their front porch for me. Bye. Love you."

"Bye," Mary and Bradley called as the door closed quickly behind Clarissa.

Once the door closed, Mary turned back to Bradley. "I would really like to go to your high school reunion," she said, and then she sent him a sly glance. "Unless you're ashamed to introduce me to your former classmates."

"You know that's ridiculous," Bradley said. "I'm just… I'm just uncomfortable. I haven't seen them in years."

"Since Jeannine went missing," she said.

He sighed and nodded. "Yeah, since then."

"It's time to go back," she said, unwrapping a strand of webs from his neck and replacing them with her arms. "Besides, I love the idea of dancing the night away in your arms."

He wrapped her in his arms and bent his head to give her a real kiss. But as he bent down, a fuzzy, rubber bat dropped from his head onto the floor. He looked at the bat and looked at Mary who was trying to stifle her laughter. "Okay, we'll go," he said. "But only if you can get this stuff off of me in time."

Chapter Four

When Mary walked out of the bathroom, Bradley turned and stared at her.

"What?" she asked, backing toward the bathroom. "Do I have spinach in my teeth? Is my blouse on inside out?"

He smiled and shook his head, stepping across the room and grasping her arm before she could go any farther. "I am just totally amazed at how, at seven months pregnant, you can still be the sexiest woman I've ever seen," he said, shaking his head in wonder.

A wide smile spread across her face. "Well, that was the nicest thing I've heard today," she replied, reaching up and giving him a kiss. "Thank you. And no, we are not going to stay home."

He sighed. "Okay, I wasn't lying about how you look, but do we really have to go?" he asked.

"Mike said it was important," she replied.

"Mike?" Bradley asked. "Why would Mike say it was important for us to go to my high school reunion?"

"Search me," she said. "But if he feels we should go…"

Bradley nodded. "Yeah, we should go."

It took them a little over an hour to drive to the high school in Sycamore. "Are we going to be late?" Mary asked as they pulled into the lot.

Looking around the nearly empty parking lot, Bradley shook his head. "Maybe we have the wrong night," he said. He drove the car over to the doors that led to the gym and noticed a large sign on the door.

"School closed due to water main break. Reunion moved to Brown's Grocery store at the site of East State Street High School."

"Okay, this is not a good idea," Bradley said.

"Why not?" Mary asked, reading over his shoulder. "I think it's cool that they're having the dance in a grocery store."

Turning to face her in the car, he said, "It's not a good idea because the old high school was built over a cemetery, and even after the high school was torn down and the grocery store built on top of it, there were stories about paranormal events."

Mary bit back a smile and widened her eyes. "Oh, no! Ghosts!" she exclaimed. "I don't know if I could take seeing a ghost." She dramatically laid the back of her hand against her forehead and leaned back. "It's just too much for my sensitive disposition."

"Funny," Bradley replied, clearly not as amused as Mary thought he ought to be. "But picture this. You and I in a large building surrounded by potentially hundreds of spirits all vying for your attention."

"See, that's the beauty of it," she explained. "When I'm in your arms, the spirits don't come after me. So, I have a wonderful excuse to be close to you all night long."

"What about the bathroom?" he asked. "We both know you're going to be spending some time in there."

She grinned. "I think I can handle it," she said. "And if not, I promise I'll ask you to take me home."

"Promise?" he asked.

She nodded. "Scout's honor."

Bradley drove the car out of the parking lot and headed towards downtown Sycamore. Mary looked out the window at the picturesque town passing before her eyes. "It must have been great growing up here," she said.

Bradley nodded. "Yeah, I have a lot of great memories," he said. "My dad was kind of a small town boy wonder; it was great walking in his shadow."

She turned and faced him. "Really?" she asked. "What was he like?"

"He was the quarterback on the football team, the pitcher on the baseball team and the forward on the basketball team," he said. "And even though it could have gone to his head, he was a nice, humble guy who was always willing to help someone out."

"Did he look like you?" she asked.

Bradley nodded. "Yeah, he and I look nearly identical," he said.

"Well, that must have been trouble," she replied.

"Why?" he asked, clearly confused.

"He looked like you, he was a star athlete, and he was nice?" she asked. "The girls must have been battling for his attention."

Chuckling, Bradley turned into the parking lot next to the grocery store. "Well, don't worry," he said. "The charm stayed with that generation. I was the nerdy, swim team guy. The girls didn't look twice at me."

Mary shook her head. "Bradley Alden, either you're lying to me, the girls here were all blind, or you were just totally unaware of what went on around you."

Chapter Five

Bradley had been totally unaware of what was going on around him, Mary decided after they walked into the building. Although he opened the door for her and had her enter first, Mary was partially hidden as they entered the empty grocery store now festooned with crepe paper and balloons. She watched as many of the women in the room became aware of Bradley's arrival and quickly whispered to a friend next to them, causing a chain reaction of wide-eyed, interested females. Smiling, in a predatory way only other women understood, a few of them began to move toward him.

That's my cue, Mary thought, and stepping up next to him, she slipped her arm possessively around his. He looked down at her, still unaware of the feminine machinations going on around him, and smiled tenderly. "Are you okay?" he asked.

"I'm just great," she smiled back, a little ashamed to acknowledge her feeling of delight at being partnered with, in her humble opinion, the best-looking man in the room. "Why don't you introduce me to your friends?"

Bradley looked up and glanced around the room, searching for a familiar face. But before he completely scanned the crowd, a booming male voice resounded next to them. "Why if it isn't Bradley

Alden! And here I thought you were dead," he laughed at his own joke.

Mary felt Bradley's arm tense underneath her own. She turned and looked at the balding, slightly paunchy man dressed in a Sycamore High School sweatshirt and jeans.

"Hi, Neil, how are you?" Bradley asked politely.

Mary bit back a smile; Bradley only treated people he really didn't like with that much courtesy.

"I'm great, just great," Neil said, hitching up his pants as he spoke. "You know I've moved into a management position at the dealership. If you are ever looking for a sweet deal on a car..."

"It was nice seeing you, Neil," Bradley said, stepping forward with Mary.

"Hey, wait," Neil said, moving over to block Bradley's escape. "I haven't paid my respects to the little woman." He smiled at Mary, taking a long moment to check out her body and then, finally, meeting her eyes. "Jeannine, right? I never forget a name or a face. I think you were pregnant the last time I saw you. You and the Brad man trying to populate the entire world on your own?"

Mary glanced up at Bradley for help.

"Actually, this is my wife, Mary," Bradley corrected. "Jeannine died eight years ago. Now, if you'll excuse us." Bradley guided Mary around Neil, who was actually momentarily speechless, and moved her across the room.

"Well, he was charming," Mary whispered to Bradley, a teasing smile in her eyes.

Bradley released a pent-up sigh and shook his head. "Mary, I am so sorry."

"You are not responsible for the actions of your former classmates," she said. "And really, he did you a favor."

"What?" Bradley asked, looking down at her.

Mary nodded her head back in the direction they'd come from, and they both saw Neil busy at work, gossiping and not-so-subtly pointing in their direction. "You won't have to explain about me or Jeannine to anyone else," she said.

"It's none of their damn business," Bradley replied stiffly.

"It's human nature to be interested in the lives of people you know," she said. "And I know you guys on the police force talk about people in town all the time."

He shrugged, slightly embarrassed. "Well, that's professional gossip," he improvised.

27

"Yeah, right," she laughed. "Professional only means you're better at it than anyone else."

This time he laughed and nodded. "Well, we try our best."

"Bradley. Bradley Alden. You come on over here and talk to me."

Chapter Six

Mary and Bradley turned and saw the elderly woman standing in the corner of the store. She was a tiny woman with gray hair, spectacles perched on an upturned nose, and sparkling green eyes. She was dressed in a slim skirt and a high-collared, button-up blouse.

"Mrs. Penfield," Bradley exclaimed softly as they moved over to speak to her. "I'm really surprised to see you."

She smiled up at him. "Well, of course I had to come and check up on all of my former students," she replied, and then she looked from Bradley to Mary. "You got the pick of the litter when it comes to the rest of the young men in his graduating class."

Mary smiled back at the elderly teacher. "I agree with you," she said. "What courses did you teach?"

"Mrs. Penfield was my English and Literature teacher," Bradley said. "She made Shakespeare come alive in our class."

"It only came alive to those who were willing to pay attention," she said with an approving nod in Bradley's direction. "And this one always paid attention."

"Yes, he's very good at attention to detail," Mary agreed.

"I also taught young Alden's father," the teacher explained. "Alike in many ways. But I admit, the younger was always my favorite."

Bradley blushed. "Mrs. Penfield, thank you," he said. "But, really, you don't have to say that."

"I'm only telling the truth," she said. "Now don't get me wrong. Your father was a good man. But there was something about you..." she paused for a moment. "More depth of character. More looking below the surface, not taking things for granted."

Smiling up at him, she shook her head. "You were always just a nice young man," she finished.

"Thank you," he said. "And you were always my favorite teacher."

She looked over at Mary and winked. "You need to watch out for him," she said. "He was always a charmer."

"Well, he certainly charmed me," Mary said with a smile.

Mrs. Penfield leaned closer to Mary. "If you ever need to talk to me about this young man, you come and see me," she said, a twinkle in her eye. "I spend a lot of time at the Joiner Room at the library. You can almost always find me there."

"I'll remember that," Mary said.

"Hey," Bradley inserted. "I would think by now most of that would be beyond the statute of limitations."

Mary shook her head. "Oh, no, when you're married, there is no statute of limitations."

Mrs. Penfield chuckled. "I do like your wife, Bradley," she said. "She's got spunk."

Bradley nodded. "Yes, she does," he said. "And I am never bored with her around."

"That's lovely," the elderly teacher replied, her eyes getting soft with tenderness. "That's an important asset in a marriage."

She sighed gently. "I still remember my dear husband…"

"Bradley. Bradley Alden," the young woman squealed. "I can't believe you're here!"

She walked through the old woman, and with a soft sigh, the elderly teacher's spirit disappeared. Pausing for a moment, the woman wrapped her hands around her bare arms and shivered. "Oh, I just got a chill," she complained.

"This was probably the old freezer section," Mary said wryly.

The not-all-that-natural blonde glanced in Mary's direction for a passing moment and sent her a wan smile, then turned her obvious charms in Bradley's direction. Bradley stepped back, so those charms didn't brush up against him.

"Hi," the blonde breathlessly offered. "It's been so long."

Bradley shook his head. "I'm so sorry," he said dispassionately. "But I can't seem to remember you."

Mary nearly choked.

The blonde eyebrows went up as far as her plastic surgery would allow. "You don't remember me?" she asked, clearly taken aback.

Bradley shrugged easily. "Nope, sorry."

"I was the homecoming queen," she retorted.

The music started playing in the background, a slow, romantic song. Bradley looked down at Mary and smiled, his eyes smoldering. "You promised you'd let me hold you in my arms," he said softly.

Mary smiled back at him. "I never break a promise," she replied, her heart skipping a beat.

He turned back to the confused blonde. "Congratulations on being homecoming queen," he said. "But you'll have to excuse me; I'm going to dance with my wife."

He guided Mary onto the dance floor and pulled her close, their bodies swaying slowly to the music.

"I think you broke her heart," Mary whispered, laying her head on Bradley's shoulder.

"Nicole Kohler doesn't have a heart," he replied softly, his breath tickling her ear.

Mary lifted her head and looked up in surprise. "You knew who she was?"

Bradley placed a light kiss on her lips. "Mmmmm-hmmmm," he murmured. "But I didn't like the way she treated you."

She smiled, sighed, and then snuggled back against his chest. "You are my hero."

Chuckling lightly, he laid his head on hers. "And you are the sexiest woman in the room."

"You looked at all the other women?" she asked. She tried to lift her head, but he kept it trapped with his own.

Time to change the direction of this conversation, Bradley decided.

"So, I thought when we were together, ghosts were kept away," he said.

She smiled, knowing exactly what he was trying to do and deciding to play along with it. "That's only if the ghosts are trying to contact me," she said. "But Mrs. Penfield was here looking for you. What a sweet woman."

"Yeah, you didn't have to take her tests," Bradley grumbled. "She wasn't so sweet back in the day."

"I wonder if she was the reason we had to come tonight," Mary mused.

"Does that mean we can leave?" Bradley asked, a note of optimism in his voice.

Mary laughed softly. "One more slow song," she said as she snuggled closer to him with a satisfied sigh. "And then we can go."

He guided her in a slow turn in the corner of the dance floor where the glaring, grocery store fluorescent lights had been turned off and only dim light guided their steps. The music was slow, bluesy and romantic, with just enough sexual suggestion in the lyrics to be enticing.

"One more song?" he asked, his warm breath sending shivers down her spine.

She sighed. "I love dancing with you," she said. "So I hate to go."

"Well, we could continue this song at home," he whispered, his voice slightly hoarse. "In our bedroom."

She felt the heat immediately, her breathing shallow and her heart hammering. Looking up at him, her eyes soft with desire, she slowly moistened her dry lips with her tongue. "Maybe we should leave now," she breathed.

He looked down at her and nodded. "Yeah," he agreed. "Right now."

Chapter Seven

Bradley placed his hand on the small of Mary's back and guided her off the dance floor and toward the entrance. "Only a few more steps and we'll be…"

"Bradley. Bradley Alden," a male voice called from behind them.

Bradley stopped and turned. "Rick? Rick Thomas, is that you?"

Mary turned and watched Bradley embrace a tall, dark-haired man. "It's been too long," Rick said. "I thought you were out of state."

Nodding, Bradley shrugged. "I was, for a while," he explained. "Then I got a job in Freeport and…" He turned towards Mary. "Mary, this is Rick Thomas. Rick, this is my wife, Mary. Rick went to high school with me, and then we were in the service together. He re-upped and I went home." Then he turned back to Rick. "I met Mary when I was working on a case in Freeport." He glanced at Mary and smiled. "Best case I ever worked on."

Rick chuckled. "I can see that."

"Hi," Mary said, coming forward and shaking Rick's hand. "It's good to meet you."

Rick smiled back. "The pleasure is all mine," he replied. "When is the baby due?"

"January," she said. "So, we only have a few more months to go."

"Wow, you're going to be a dad," Rick said to Bradley. "How does that make you feel?"

"Well, actually, I'm already a dad," he said. "Clarissa is eight years old, nearly nine. And she keeps us hopping."

Shaking his head, Rick looked from Bradley to Mary. "Wait," he said. "That's right. You and Jeannine were married. What happened?"

Before Bradley could explain, Mary placed her hand on Bradley's arm. "I need to find the lady's room," she said. "So take your time with Rick. I'll find you when I'm done." She smiled over at Rick. "Nice meeting you."

"You, too," he said.

Rick turned to see Bradley watching Mary, a concerned look on his face. "Hey, it's just a trip to the bathroom," he teased. "I'm sure she'll be fine. I don't think the ghosts of East High will accost her."

Surprised, Bradley turned back to his friend. "What?" he asked. "The ghosts of East High?"

Rick chuckled. "Wow, you have it bad," he said, patting Bradley's shoulder. "She'll be fine; the bathroom is only a few yards away."

Taking a deep breath, Bradley nodded. "Yeah, you're right," he said. "I just worry about her."

"So, you were going to tell me about Jeannine," Rick prompted.

"Right," Bradley said. "Well, it's a long story."

Mary stopped and looked over her shoulder at Bradley and Rick before she went into the bathroom. Bradley was talking and Rick was nodding slowly, his face filled with sympathy. *They must be talking about Jeannine*, she thought.

She turned back around and found herself surrounded by people. Dead people.

"Can you see me?" a young man in buckskin asked.

"Do you know where I am?" an older woman dressed in 19th century shroud asked.

"I'm looking for my mommy and daddy," a little girl in a long dress and pinafore cried.

Hundreds of spirits, mostly from the early years of the town of Sycamore, came forward from all directions toward Mary, each with a request. She looked around, feeling a little panicked. She thought about answering their questions, turning them towards the light, but there were just too many of them to deal with.

Mary could no longer see the walls of the grocery store; all she could see were layer upon layer of spirits trying to get her attention. Crowding in closer and closer. Crying, shouting and pleading for her help. She tried to move, tried to back away and get back to Bradley, but the throngs were too deep and the air seemed thick.

"I've got to get out of here," she murmured. "I can't breathe."

She tried to move forward but stumbled, the throng moving up against her. "Please," she whispered to the ghosts. "Please, I have to sit down. I'm feeling faint."

But they were so caught up in their own needs, they didn't hear her quiet pleas.

"I wonder if someone can be crushed by a stampede of ghosts," she murmured vaguely as the room started to spin around her. She looked around helplessly as the darkness closed in. "I think I'm going to faint."

Chapter Eight

Bradley was at Mary's side before she hit the ground, wrapping his arms around her and holding her up. "Mary," he said, his voice shaking with concern. "Mary, what's wrong."

She trembled in his arms, took a shaky breath and slowly opened her eyes. "Hey," she breathed softly. "I think I fainted."

Bradley took a deep, calming breath and nodded. "Yeah. Yeah, I think you did, too," he said, trying to get the nerves out of his voice. "And now, the million dollar question is why?"

She tried to look around, but Bradley was holding her too tight for her to move. "Are we in a crowd?" she whispered.

Looking around, he nodded. "Yes," he whispered back. "We've got company."

"Oh, how awkward," she replied, biting her lower lip. "Can we just blame it on pregnancy?"

He met her eyes. "Was it?" he asked.

"No," she said softly. "It was more, um, paranormal than that."

He nodded slowly. "I'm so sorry. I should have remembered about the cemetery. I should have never let you go alone."

This time a wide smile spread over her face as she looked at him. "Really? I think you walking into the ladies room with me would have been slightly more awkward than me getting a little lightheaded," she teased.

"Maybe we're one of those couples who can't bear to be separated from each other," he suggested with a twinkle in his eyes.

She grinned. "Or maybe we're just plain weird."

Chuckling softly, he nodded. "Maybe we are," he said and then studied her for a moment. "Are you okay now?"

"Yes, I'm feeling much better now that the crowd is gone," she replied. "I think you can let me go."

He loosened his hold, and she stepped away from him.

"Are you okay?" Rick asked.

Mary nodded. "Yeah, it's just a pregnancy thing," she said casually. "Little Mikey likes to cut off my circulation, and I get a little lightheaded."

"I feel so bad," Rick said. "Bradley was watching you, and I was teasing him. I had no idea that you could actually be in trouble."

Mary smiled up at Bradley, her heart in her eyes. "You were watching out for me?" she asked.

Bradley shrugged. "It was no big deal," he replied, embarrassed.

"No big deal," Rick said. "He saw you stumble, and he was across the room in a flash."

"My hero, again," she said. "I guess I'm going to have to keep you."

He nodded. "Yeah, you have no choice in the matter there," he replied with a smile. Then he turned to Rick. "I'm going to get her home. I've got your number, so I'll give you a call. Okay?"

"Yeah, that would be great," Rick said. "Nice to meet you, Mary."

"You too, Rick," she replied. She started to turn and stopped, noticing the ghost of a teen-aged girl standing next to Rick. The blonde-haired girl with a beehive hairstyle was dressed in a simple peach-colored sleeveless sheath dress that reached down to her knees adorned with a satin ribbon at the empress waistline. But the sadness she wore on her face was what drew Mary's attention. *There must be a powerful reason for her to speak with me,* Mary thought, *if she is able to push through Bradley's ghost blocking abilities.*

Only thinking of the girl, Mary smiled in her direction. "What's your name?" she asked.

The girl didn't respond, but continued to gaze in their direction. Unfortunately, Rick heard Mary and thought she was speaking to him. "It's Rick," he said to Mary, speaking slowly and precisely. "Rick Thomas. Bradley's friend."

I feel like such an idiot, Mary thought, a blush creeping across her face.

"I'm sorry, Rick," she apologized. "There was someone behind you that I was speaking to, but they're gone now."

His smile didn't quite reach his eyes, and he nodded. "Oh, well, that makes sense."

Yes, he thinks I'm nuts, Mary thought with a soft sigh.

"Mary sees ghosts," Bradley inserted casually.

Turning to Bradley in surprise, Mary sent him a shocked look. "What?" she asked.

Grinning, Bradley nodded in Rick's direction. "Rick grew up in a haunted house," he said. "He saw stuff all the time."

Breathing a sigh of relief, Mary turned back to him. "Really? You see ghosts?" she asked.

He shrugged, obviously uncomfortable with the conversation in the midst of his former classmates. "Would you like me to walk both of you to the car?" he asked.

Mary nodded. "That would be nice."

"Don't you need to…?" Bradley cocked his head towards the bathroom.

"Not in that one," Mary replied with a wry smile. "We can stop at a gas station on the way home."

Chapter Nine

"Okay, that was crazy that your best friend in high school saw ghosts," Mary said to Bradley as they drove west on Highway 20 towards Freeport.

"He wasn't quite as open about it as you are," Bradley said with a smile. "As a matter of fact, he never mentioned it until tonight."

She turned from looking out the window and stared at her husband driving the car. "Tonight?" she asked. "How did that just drop into the conversation?"

He shrugged. "I was telling him about you and how I met you," he said. "And about Earl."

The reminder of Bradley's first encounter with a ghost still made her chuckle. "You were so adorable," she teased. "All Chuck Norris and Charlie's Angels wrapped up in one."

He turned to her, his mouth in a grimace. "Really? Charlie's Angels?" he asked. "Couldn't you have just left it with Chuck Norris?"

Chuckling, she shook her head. "Okay, let me try again," she laughed. "All Chuck Norris and Clint Eastwood wrapped up in one." She schooled her features so they looked as serious as she could muster and tried to mimic the famous actor. "So, ghost, do you feel lucky? Well, do you?"

"I don't think you're taking my manly moves and nerves of steel seriously," he replied, biting back a smile.

"I took them very seriously," she said. "Until you broke my favorite cookie jar."

He chuckled. "I had never even considered that ghosts were real," he said. "My whole world was turned upside down when I met you."

She reached over and placed her hand on his arm. "Yeah, so was mine," she said seductively.

He looked down at her hand and then up into her eyes, and she shivered at the heat in them. "Good thing we stopped for gas and bathroom before we got on the highway," he said seriously. "Because we are headed straight home."

Grinning at him, she nodded. "You'll hear no complaints from me," she said. "I want to get you home, Mr. Alden, and take total advantage of you."

"I really like it when you talk that way," he replied with a smile.

"Ouch," Mary cried out, looking over her shoulder.

"What's wrong?" Bradley asked, slowing down as he took the Freeport exit.

Rubbing the back of her neck, Mary shook her head. "My hair must have caught in my zipper or the headrest or something," she said. "Because something just pulled my hair."

"Are you okay?" he asked.

She nodded. "I'm fine," she said, still rubbing her scalp. "No big deal, just a little surprising."

A few minutes later Bradley pulled the car into the driveway, then came around to help Mary get out of the car. With one hand braced on the car and the other on Bradley's arm, Mary was able to push herself into a standing position. With a wry shake of her head, she turned to her husband. "A couple more months and we're going to need a block and tackle to get me out of the car," she said.

He nodded, as if he were seriously considering the matter. "I've actually been thinking about installing a lift chair in the car," he replied, biting back a smile. "You could press a button, and the seat would eject you." He mimicked the sideways action with his hand. "Poof, you're out of the car."

Placing her hands on her hips, she stared at him. "Oh, that's a great idea," she replied sarcastically. "Not!"

She started to walk slowly toward the house, then turned and looked over her shoulder. "Um, what happened to the charming Mr. Alden that I was dancing with earlier?" she asked. "Hmmmm, I must have left him in Sycamore."

Chuckling, Bradley hurried to her side and kissed her cheek. "He had a momentary lapse," he said. "Of course an ejection seat wouldn't work."

"Thank you," she said.

"Yeah, the angles are all wrong," he teased. Placing his arm under her elbow, he guided her up the stairs.

"Just one day," she said, as she caught her breath at the top of the stairs. "If you were pregnant for just one day..."

"I would be a total wimp," he confessed, unlocking the door for both of them. "I don't know how you put up with it or me."

They walked inside and he closed the door behind them. Mary turned and looped her arms around his neck. "Well," she sighed dramatically, "if you weren't so darn good-looking, I would have a really hard time."

He bent forward and kissed her. "Lucky for me I've still got my looks," he said, nibbling his way from her lips down to the side of her neck.

She moaned softly. "Oh, and you do that really well," she said, closing her eyes and enjoying the sparks traveling through her body.

A loud crash had them jumping apart. "What in the world…" Bradley exclaimed.

"It came from the kitchen," Mary said as she moved across the room.

They crossed the living room and turned into the kitchen. "Oh, no," Mary exclaimed as she saw the cookie jar Bradley had bought her to replace the one he'd broken lying in pieces on the floor. "How did that happen?"

She started to moved forward, and Bradley stopped her. "I'll clean it up," he said. "There's a little too much bending over for you."

"Are you sure?" she asked.

He smiled at her. "I'm pretty good at cleaning up cookie jars up from off this kitchen floor."

She smiled back and then glanced around the room. "It's so weird," she said. "It's been in that same spot on the counter for months. Why would it just slip off now?"

Bradley shrugged and then smiled. "Maybe it was haunted," he said, wiggling his eyebrows.

"Oh, don't even joke about that," Mary said, unconsciously rubbing her back.

Bradley walked over to her, placed a kiss on her forehead and turned her towards the living room.

"Go upstairs and put your feet up," he said. "I'll clean this up and join you in a few minutes. Okay?"

She smiled back at him. "Okay," she said. "And thank you."

She crossed the living room and started up the stairs. Then she stopped and listened. "Bradley?" she called.

"Yes?" he called back.

"Did you say something?"

"No," he replied. "Why?"

She shook her head. "I could swear I just heard someone laugh," she said, a slight shiver running up her spine.

"It was probably the broom across the tile floor and the glass shards," he suggested.

She took a deep breath and nodded. "That makes sense," she replied, nodding. "Okay, I'll see you upstairs."

Chapter Ten

Walking down the upstairs hallway, Mary jumped when Mike appeared next to her.

"Sorry," he immediately apologized. "I didn't mean to scare you."

She shook her head. "No, not your fault," she said. "I'm just a little jumpy tonight."

He hovered next to her and nodded. "Yeah, about that," he said.

She recognized the tone in his voice. "Mike, what's going on?"

"Well, the reason you needed to go to the reunion tonight wasn't quite what I thought," he admitted.

She sat down on a window seat in the hall and looked up at him. "What did you think?"

"I thought Bradley needed to finish something," he said. "A little closure after Jeannine's death."

"But that wasn't it, was it?" she asked.

Suddenly her bedroom door flew open with a powerful crash. "What the...?" she exclaimed.

51

Mike nodded. "Yeah, well see, that's the problem," he said with a sigh. "You brought someone home with you tonight."

"What?"

"And it looks like she's not real happy about your relationship with Bradley," he said.

"I have a jealous ghost in my house?" Mary asked, astonished.

Mike shook his head apologetically. "No, sweetheart," he said. "You have a jealous poltergeist in your home."

As if on cue, the drawers in Mary's dresser opened, and her clothing started flying across the room. Mary turned back to Mike. "Really?" she asked. "Like I need this now?"

"I'm really sorry, Mary," he replied. "I don't know if it helps, but there is a reason for this."

Sighing, she watched as the blankets on her bed were lifted up and strewn across the room. "So, obviously poltergeists don't play by the same rules as your regular, run-of-the-mill ghosts," she said, "or she wouldn't be in my bedroom."

Mike shrugged. "Think of her as an angry teenager," he said, "with an attitude…who's got PMS."

"Crap!" Mary replied and pushed herself up to standing. "Okay, well, maybe we start with some tough love."

She walked into the center of her bedroom and immediately was hit in the face by a pair of her own underwear. And this time she was sure of it. She heard a giggle, and then suddenly the entire room was filling with swirling clothing.

"Okay," Mary said, batting the clothes away as they flew towards her. "It's obvious that you have a problem, and I'm willing to be reasonable. But throwing my clothes around the room is not going to help."

The giggle was louder, and the clothes swirled even faster. Mary couldn't move fast enough to bat them away, and in a few moments, her face was covered with several layers of clothing. She pulled at the layers to catch her breath. "Stop…" she tried to call out, but was inundated with more clothes.

"Mary, get out of there," Mike called.

She tried to move, but clothing wrapped around her legs, pinning her in place. "I…can't…" she yelled, ripping the fabric away so she could breathe. "Get…"

"What the hell is going on in here?" Bradley yelled from the doorway, and immediately all the clothing dropped to the floor.

Mary took a slow, shuddering breath, kicked the clothes away from her legs and turned towards him. Suddenly, the ghost Mary had seen standing next to Rick appeared next to Bradley.

"I'm so sorry," she whispered sadly, translucent tears flowing down her cheek. And then she faded away.

Bradley turned to Mary. "What just happened?" he asked.

"I think I just met one of your former girlfriends," she said, pulling a pair of underwear from out of her neckline. "And I don't think she was very happy to meet me."

Chapter Eleven

"A blonde with a beehive hairstyle?" Bradley asked, shaking his head as he, Mary and Mike talked about the ghost a little while later. "I don't know. Maybe she was in the high school play, or maybe she died on Halloween? I really don't remember her."

Pulling a t-shirt off the bedpost and folding it, Mary sighed. "Poor thing," she said. "She obviously remembers you and is still in love."

"Poor thing?" Bradley asked, his voice rising in anger, pulling a pair of slacks from the ceiling fan. "She nearly suffocated you with your own clothes, and you think she's a poor thing?"

"Well, a very jealous and slightly psychotic poor thing," Mary amended with a shrug, placing her shirt back in a drawer.

"Actually, poltergeists are all about emotion and drama," Mike explained. "There have been studies that often link poltergeist activity to teenage girls who are filled with emotional, um, exhilaration. Yeah, that's a good word, exhilaration."

"Wait. What? Teenaged girls filled with emotional exhilaration?" Bradley asked. "Is that normal?"

Mary and Mike looked at each other, smiled, and then looked at Bradley. "Yes," they answered together.

"But don't worry, sweetheart," Mary said. "We have at least four years until Clarissa becomes a teenager."

Bradley sighed softly. "Okay, so what are our next steps for dealing with our current teenage dilemma?"

"We need to figure out who she is," Mary said. "And hopefully her name will ring a bell." She walked across the room to pick up her laptop that was laying on the dresser. "Maybe there are some photos online," she suggested over her shoulder. She turned and reached for the laptop, but it slid across the dresser surface.

"Oh, no," she cried. "Not my laptop."

She tried to dive for it but wasn't fast enough. The laptop careened off the dresser into the wall, cracking on impact. Mary exhaled angrily. "I can't believe she did that."

Clattering behind her had Mary turning to see one of the bedside lamps being lifted off the nightstand and hung precariously in the air. She looked helplessly in Bradley's direction, and he nodded and walked over towards the nightstand.

"Hey," he said calmly. "I would really like to see you, if that's possible. I know it's been a long time."

The lamp slowly lowered to the nightstand, and the ghost appeared in the room. "She's here," Mary said. "Standing right in front of you."

"Hi," Bradley said. "In order to see you, I have to have Mary touch my arm." He shrugged. "Don't know why that works, it just does. Is it okay for Mary to come over here and touch my arm?"

The girl scowled in Mary's direction for a moment, but finally nodded.

"She said yes," Mary explained, slowly coming across the room. "But she's not too happy about it."

Mary touched Bradley's arm, and he could see the teenager standing in front of him. His anger faded as he looked at the young woman who was equally defiant and sorrowful. Her eyes were burning with unshed tears, and she was having a hard time meeting his eyes.

"You're very lovely," he said and was amazed to see a light blush appear on her translucent skin. "I don't…"

Mary squeezed his arm and, when he turned to look at her, shook her head. "Ixnay on the orgotfay," she said, looking at him meaningfully.

"What?" Bradley asked, shaking his head. "What's that?"

Mary rolled her eyes and repeated her comment slowly. "Ixnay on the orgotfay."

Bradley shook his head once more. "Sorry?"

"She said that you shouldn't tell me that you forgot me," the ghost inserted, glaring at Mary. "I speak pig Latin."

"I'm sorry," Mary said. "I didn't mean…"

"He didn't forget me," the ghost yelled, and a cold wind started whipping through the bedroom. "He wouldn't forget me. He loved me."

The lamps on the nightstand shook, and the blinds rattled. "You're just jealous," the ghost continued. "You're jealous because you're fat. Fat and ugly."

The wind increased, and the bathroom door slammed shut. "You can't have him," she screamed, and the bedroom door crashed against its frame.

The ghost disappeared, and the wind left with her.

Bradley turned to Mary. "I guess I don't know pig Latin," he admitted.

"Sorry," she replied. "I thought everyone knew pig Latin."

Bradley looked over his shoulder at the empty spot where the ghost had just stood. "Well, obviously I had a deprived childhood," he said with a smile, walking towards her. "And, by the way, you're not fat, and you're the furthest thing from ugly anyone could be."

He hugged her, and she melted into his arms. "Do you think she's gone for the night?" she asked.

He glanced around the room. "Well, it's quiet for now."

Mike glided over next to them. "I had no idea this would happen," he said. "I can make her go away if you'd like."

Mary looked over at him. "But if you did that, she wouldn't be able to return, right?" she asked. "She would never have her problem solved."

Nodding, Mike glanced around the room. "Yeah, but this is bordering on being dangerous," he said. "And you have to weigh your desire to help with the potential danger posed to your family."

"We don't have to decide tonight, do we?" she asked.

"No, you don't," Mike said, shaking his head with a gentle smile. "You really are too much of a softie."

"She just looked so sad," she replied. "And kind of lost."

"And slightly psycho," Bradley added. "But, I'm willing to give it a couple of days. As long as she doesn't threaten your safety."

Mary smiled up at him. "Okay, deal," she said.

Bradley bent down and kissed Mary. "I'm serious about the threat thing," he murmured.

"I know," she said, sighing softly and kissing him deeply. Then she stepped back. "That's why I'm going to sleep in the guest room."

"What?" Bradley exclaimed.

"Well, if her anger is egged on by jealousy, I need to keep you at a distance for a little while," she explained.

"But…" Bradley stammered. "But we were going to…." He looked over at Mike who was grinning at him and sighed. "We were going to dance."

"You owe me a…," she bit her lower lip lightly and smiled up at Bradley. "A dance. A whole night of dancing, as soon as this issue is solved."

He pulled her back into his arms and kissed her, with all the longing he was feeling. They heard shattering in the kitchen, and Bradley sighed, placing his forehead against hers. "Let's make this case top priority," he pleaded.

She sighed and nodded. "I agree."

Chapter Twelve

No sooner had Mary laid her head on the pillow in the guest room than she heard a commotion coming from inside the closet.

"We shouldn't be here," a slightly familiar female voice said.

"What? The rules said that we couldn't go into *her* bedroom," a male voice replied. "This isn't her bedroom. It's the guest room."

"Frasier, if she's sleeping in it, it's *her* bedroom," the woman replied.

Groaning softly, Mary rolled herself out of bed and padded over to the closet. As she put her hand on the doorknob she heard, "Listen Shirley, if you want to get something done these days, you've got to get in people's faces…"

Mary opened the closet door and sighed. "Okay, you're in my face now," she said. "How can I help you?"

"Look!" Shirley whispered loudly to her husband. "She's pregnant. She needs her sleep."

Frasier stared at Mary's abdomen for a moment and then looked up and met her eyes. "Hey,

I'm sorry. I didn't realize," he stammered. "Really. Go back to bed. We can talk another time."

Shaking her head, Mary pushed the door open widely and stepped back. "No, come in," she said. "It's been a crazy night, and I wasn't sure I'd be able to sleep anyway."

"Chamomile tea," Shirley said. "It helped me through each one of my pregnancies."

"She only had two," Frasier said.

"Only?" Shirley asked, her eyebrows raised in anger. "Only? And how many times have you carried a human being around in your body for nine months and then pushed it out through a tiny hole that's stretched out to be the size of a grapefruit?"

"Ouch," Mary said. "Way too much information."

Shirley turned to Mary. "Sorry," she apologized. "He just gets to me sometimes."

Frasier shrugged. "Yeah, a lot of sometimes since we've been dead."

Mary studied the two people standing in front of her. Overall they looked good, for dead people, but both of their necks were at slightly odd angles. "How did you die?" she asked.

"We drove off the side of a hill. The car crashed and rolled," Frasier explained, reaching up and rubbing his neck. "I think I broke my neck on impact."

Shirley nodded. "Yeah, we hit pretty hard," she said. "I remember the crash and then flying backwards." She paused, closed her eyes for a moment, and shuddered. "I think I must have died after the impact, too."

"Normally I don't do car accidents," Mary said.

"Well, it wasn't a normal car accident," Frasier said. "My brake lines were cut."

Shirley rolled her eyes. "You don't know that," she said. "It could have been bad brakes. You don't know someone killed us."

"If no one tried to kill us, why are we still here?" Frasier asked. "Like that angel guy, Mike, said. We got unfinished business. Bad brakes ain't unfinished business."

So, Mary thought, Mike had already talked to them about unfinished business. She wondered why Shirley was trying to find another reason.

"Who do you think killed you?" Mary asked Frasier.

"I don't think. I know," Frasier replied sadly. "My son, Eddie."

"Your son?" Mary asked, surprised. "How do you know your son did this?"

"He doesn't know," Shirley inserted, her voice breaking. "We can't be sure."

Frasier sighed and turned to his wife. "We can't keep protecting him," he said gently. "We've protected him for too long. That's why he was able to do what he did."

Mary saw the anguish in both of their faces. "Why don't we start with the facts, and then we can go from there, okay?" she asked.

Shirley nodded. "Okay, we went to Eddie's house because he invited us for dinner," she said.

"But it wasn't dinner," Frasier added. "He was in trouble and needed money. Again."

"In trouble?" Mary asked.

"Oh, not that way," Shirley said. "He wasn't into anything nefarious—"

"Except murder," Frasier interrupted.

"We don't know he did this," Shirley argued.

"Okay, we go to his house. He asks for money. We say no. He gets angry with us and walks out of the house. Half hour later, we're on the road with no brakes," Frasier said baldly. "Maybe it was a momentary lapse. Maybe he regretted it later. But, that doesn't change things for us. We're still dead."

"Do you have any evidence linking him to your murder?" Mary asked.

Frasier shook his head. "No, they just figured I fell asleep at the wheel," he said with disgust. "Like I would risk my sweetheart's life and drive drowsy. They didn't even bother checking the car."

Mary nodded and then tried to stifle a yawn. "Oh, I'm so sorry," she said.

"No, we're the ones who should be sorry," Shirley replied. "You need your sleep. We can wait."

"Well, tomorrow is Sunday, so most of the places I need to check won't be open until Monday morning," she said. "My computer had a slight mishap this evening, but I'll ask my husband to start checking into some things, okay?"

"Thank you," Frasier said. "If you have any questions…"

Shirley smiled sadly. "We'll just be hanging around, waiting."

"I'll let you know as soon as I have any information," Mary said. "And you might want to think about anyone else who could be a suspect. Just in case Eddie is cleared."

"That would be nice," Frasier admitted. "And we'll start thinking about it."

Chapter Thirteen

Mary was surprised that the sun was fairly high in the sky when she woke up the next morning. Turning to the bedside clock, she gasped in surprise when she saw that it was after nine. "Good grief," she muttered, leveraging herself out of bed. "Why didn't anyone wake me up?"

She opened the guest room door and turned when she heard footsteps on the stairs.

"Well, good morning, sleepyhead," Bradley said as he carried a mug of tea in her direction. "I was just coming up to see you."

"I can't believe I slept this long," she replied.

"Well, I've heard that fighting a poltergeist when you're seven months pregnant can be exhausting," he said, bending down and kissing her. "And I would have let you sleep even longer, but I just got a call from Rosie. They're coming over in about an hour, and they're bringing a friend."

"A friend?" Mary asked.

"A friend of Rosie's who's going to be staying with them for a while," Bradley replied. "She had hip surgery and needs some convalescing time."

"Well, if I needed some convalescing time, there's no one I'd rather do it with than Rosie," Mary said. Then she thought about it. "Of course, I'd end up gaining ten pounds."

Chuckling, Bradley walked with Mary to their bedroom. She paused at the doorway and peeked inside. "Any sign of…" Mary whispered, looking around the room, "anything?"

Bradley shook his head. "No, it's been quiet all morning," he replied.

"Yeah, well, I haven't been in the picture either," Mary said.

Nodding, Bradley walked into the bedroom first. "Yeah, I thought of that, too," he said. "So, I'll just stay close while you get dressed, just to make sure she doesn't try anything."

Mary quickly glanced around, then rose up on her tiptoes and kissed him. "Thank you," she said. "You're my hero."

True to her word, about an hour later, Rosie and Stanley arrived with their guest, Margo Taylor. She had a warm and winning smile, and Mary liked her immediately. In a few minutes they were seated at the kitchen table enjoying Rosie's famous blueberry muffins and cups of tea.

"So, how did you meet?" Mary asked just before she popped a warm piece of muffin into her mouth.

"Well, I went to Deadwood for a convention about ten years ago," Rosie said, "and I met Margo. She lives there."

"You live in Deadwood? South Dakota?" Bradley asked. "And you came to Freeport to recover from surgery?"

Margo smiled at him. "Well, there are a lot fewer hills here and less snow," she replied. "Besides, I haven't had a chance to visit with Rosie for ages, and I thought, why not?"

"We invited her down for the wedding," Stanley said. "But she couldn't get away. It was a busy time of year for her daughter."

"Oh, what does your daughter do?" Mary asked.

Margo smiled. "I was hoping you'd ask," she said. "She's a famous mystery writer. Ann Charles."

Mary sat back in her chair and stared, open-mouthed, at Margo. "Are you kidding?" she exclaimed. "You're Ann Charles' mom? I love her books."

"And Margo is something of an amateur sleuth herself," Rosie replied. "So if you need any help on cases this week…"

"Oh, do you do detective work?" Margo asked.

"Yes, I'm a private investigator," Mary replied. "I specialize in certain kinds of cases."

"What kinds?" Margo asked, intrigued.

Mary took a deep breath and was about to try to explain what she did when Rosie turned to her friend. "Oh, Mary can see ghosts. So she helps solve their murders."

Margo nodded, picked up her tea and sipped. "Well, that's interesting," she said calmly.

"You don't think that's weird?" Bradley asked.

Margo smiled at him. "Oh, sweetie, I'm from Deadwood," she said. "There's not much on this earth that strikes me as weird."

Chapter Fourteen

Mary sat back on the couch, comfortably resting against Bradley's arm, and watched Rosie visit with Margo. They had so many stories about their adventures together, each one more hilarious than the last. She loved to see Rosie so obviously happy, and even Stanley got into the act sharing some of his own Rosie stories.

"Did she ever show you her emergency bag?" Stanley asked.

"The one with the blow-up doll?" Margo replied with a chuckle.

"The very same," Stanley said. "I never, ever met a woman who carried so much stuff with her."

"Well, one never knows when one might have an emergency situation," Rosie defended herself. "Besides, it came in very handy, didn't it, Mary?"

Mary smiled and nodded, remembering how the blow-up doll had taken her place at her desk, throwing one of Bradley's officers off her scent while she escaped to solve a crime.

Bradley cleared his throat and shook his head. "I didn't think it was funny," he said.

Mary reached up and kissed his jaw. "I remember."

Mary was about to make another comment when the front door burst open and Clarissa and Maggie came running inside. "Hi!" Clarissa called her cheeks pink from the cold. "Do I smell blueberry muffins?"

"Clarissa, did you forget to greet Rosie and Stanley?" Bradley asked. "And this is their friend, Mrs. Taylor."

Clarissa smiled. "Hi, Aunt Rosie, Uncle Stanley and Mrs. Taylor," she replied politely. "Um, Aunt Rosie…"

Rosie laughed. "Yes, I did make blueberry muffins, and yes, you and Maggie may have some. Actually, I brought extra for Maggie's family if you want to bring them over."

"That would be so cool," Maggie replied eagerly. "Thank you."

"Yeah, I was just coming to get more clothes," Clarissa said. "And my homework."

"What?" Mary asked, turning to Bradley.

"I'm sorry," Bradley said, wincing slightly. "I forgot to tell you. Because of the case you are working on," he said meaningfully, "I thought it might be better if Clarissa spent a couple of nights with the Brennans. I called while you were still sleeping, and I forgot to tell you."

Mary opened her mouth and then closed it. It really did make perfect sense. She didn't know how dangerous the poltergeist could be.

"I'm really sorry," Bradley said quietly.

Mary shook her head. "No. No, it's fine," she said. "It makes perfect sense, but I just feel bad about it."

Clarissa came across the room and gave Mary a hug. "Don't feel bad," she said. "We're actually helping Mrs. Brennan do stuff."

Mary kissed Clarissa and hugged her back. "Well, as long as you're helping, I'll try not to miss you too much."

Clarissa looked up at her mom and smiled. "You can miss me," she said. "And I'll miss you, too."

"Deal," Mary replied, feeling a little misty eyed. "I love you."

"I love you, too," Clarissa replied softly. "Is it okay if I go?"

Mary nodded. "Yes, it's more than okay," she said. "Do you need help carrying things?"

"No," Maggie said with a broad grin. "I just called Andy and told him about the muffins. He's coming over to help carry stuff home."

Mary laughed. "The sure way to the Brennan boys' hearts is through their stomachs."

A few minutes later the girls, Clarissa's things and the muffins were on their way over to the Brennan's.

"Mary," Margo asked, leaning forward in her chair. "What's this case you're working on? If you don't mind me asking."

Deciding it would be better not to mention the poltergeist, Mary said, "It's the possible murder of an older couple whose car might have been tampered with," she said. "Their names are Shirley and Frasier, but I don't…"

"Shirley and Frasier Koch?" Stanley asked. "Died about six months ago in a car accident?"

Mary nodded. "That sounds about right," she said. "But they hadn't given me their last name."

"Oh, I met them," Rosie said. "They went to the VFW dinners. Frasier was a friend of Stanley's."

"Are you saying they were killed?" Stanley asked.

"That's what they believe," Mary said. "But I haven't had a chance to start looking into it yet."

"Do they have any suspects?" Margo asked.

75

"I really don't want to speculate until I've done more research," Mary replied.

"It's always the ones you least suspect," Margo replied sagely. Then she turned to Stanley. "Maybe we could brainstorm a list of people you both knew who could be potential suspects."

Stanley turned to Mary. "Well, I don't want to step on anyone's toes," he said.

Shaking her head, Mary smiled. "No, you would be helping. Thank you," she said. "I could use the help. My computer is out of commission, so until it's up and running, I'm lost."

Chapter Fifteen

"Hello. Computer Dynamics, Renee speaking."

"Hi Renee, this is Mary O'Reilly-Alden," Mary said, sitting back in her office chair and relaxing as she spoke on her cell phone. "My computer crashed."

"You mean your hard drive crashed?" Renee asked.

Mary sighed. "No, my whole computer. CRASH, against the wall," Mary said.

There was a pause on the other end. "I see," Renee replied. "Well, let me fill out some paperwork here. Is this a business insurance claim?"

"Does insurance cover poltergeists?" Mary asked.

Another long pause. "Mary, why don't you just bring it in, and we'll see what we can do," Renee suggested.

Mary smiled. "Thank you, Renee," she said. "And thanks for understanding."

"I hate to admit this," Renee said with a chuckle. "But a poltergeist is not the strangest reason for a damaged computer I've heard."

Mary laughed. "Someday we need to do lunch and exchange stories."

"Yes, we do," Renee chuckled. "Yes, we do."

After she hung up the phone, Mary slipped the remains of her computer into her briefcase. "I sure hope they can resurrect you," she said.

"You're not supposed to be messing with resurrection," Mike said as he appeared next to her.

"Oh, don't worry," she said. "It's just my computer hard drive, nothing more spiritual than that."

"So, you met Shirley and Frasier?" he asked.

She nodded. "Yeah, Saturday night in the guest room closet," she said. "They seem like really nice people."

"Salt of the earth," he said. "And once they retired, they volunteered for everything: VFW, Chamber, Visitors Bureau, Women's Club. You name it, they either volunteered or ran it."

"Do you really think their son would kill them?" she asked.

Mike shrugged. "I don't know enough about him," he said. "But it sounds like the argument was pretty fierce."

Mary nodded. "Well, Bradley's running a check on him today, and Stanley, Rosie and Margo are putting together a list of other potential suspects," she said.

"And what are you doing today?" he asked.

"Once I drop off my computer, I'm heading down to Sycamore to see if I can figure out who our houseguest is," she replied. "The sooner we figure out who she is, the sooner my life can get back to somewhat normal."

Mike laughed. "Somewhat normal is right," he said. "Can you handle one more project?"

She studied him for a moment and sighed. "What is it?"

"I don't know exactly," he said. "But if you could call Bradley's friend, Rick, and have him meet you for lunch, it would be a good thing."

"A good thing as in…"

Mike shrugged. "That's all I've got," he said. "It would be a good thing."

"Okay," she nodded. "I can do a good thing." She smiled at him. "Besides, I love lunch."

"Thanks, Mary," he said. "I'll hang around the house and make sure your guest doesn't get out of line."

"Thank you," she said sincerely. "I'll be a lot less worried knowing that I will actually have a house to come back to."

He smiled at her. "Drive safely," he said as he started to fade away. "And enjoy your lunch."

Chapter Sixteen

The fields alongside the highways from Freeport to Sycamore were filled with combines harvesting corn and soybeans, like behemoth creatures lumbering across half-barren fields of stubbled brown and gold. Keeping an eye out for displaced wildlife running out into the road, Mary drove with the windows slightly open and the radio blasting, enjoying the bright autumn sun and the unusually mild weather.

As she got closer to Sycamore, fields gave way to small strip malls and residential neighborhoods with lovely old homes with big lawns and wrap-around front porches. The residential area gave way to the downtown district, with old, stately buildings and newer retail shops. She drove through the lovely downtown, much larger than Freeport's, towards the end of the district and found the distinct, red-bricked Sycamore Library.

The building was originally built in the early 1900s and had a round, turret-like corner on one end. The other end sported a recent addition made of similar red brick and newer windows. Mary walked across the parking lot into the entrance in the newer addition and found the place she was looking for right away, the Joiner Room.

She was greeted immediately when she walked into the room. "Hello," a woman behind the counter said. "I'm Sue. How can I help you?"

Mary hesitated for a moment. How in the world was she going to ask for help looking for the photo of a ghost?

Suddenly a movement in the corner of her eye caught her attention. She turned to see the ghost of an elderly man with a dapper moustache. He was smiling at her. He winked and then lifted his hand up and knocked a book off one of the upper shelves. Mary jumped in surprise.

"I'm so sorry," Sue said immediately, appearing more embarrassed than surprised. "That's Fred. One of our resident ghosts. I'm afraid he often shows off for pretty guests."

Mary smiled and turned to include Fred in her smile. "Well, I'm so glad he decided to do that," she explained coming closer to the counter. "You see, my request is, um, slightly paranormal."

The woman's smile widened. "Oh, we can handle it here," she said. "We are fairly used to handling all kinds of unusual requests."

Mary was telling her about the ghost with the beehive hairstyle when she noticed another ghost coming up behind Sue and nodding to Mary.

"Well, hello dear," Mrs. Penfield, the teacher from the reunion, greeted her. "It's so nice to see you again. May I help you find something?"

Mary smiled and tried to address her comments to both Sue and Mrs. Penfield. "I was really hoping to look through some of the old yearbooks and see if I could recognize her," Mary said.

"Of course," Sue replied, turning and pointing across the room. "The Sycamore High School yearbooks are on several shelves in that corner. I can show…"

She stopped when the door opened and several other patrons came in. Mary saw that Mrs. Penfield was already headed in the direction of the books. "I can find my way there," Mary said with a smile. "So you can help the next people."

Sue nodded. "Thank you," she said. "But if you need any help, don't hesitate to ask."

Mary slipped down the aisle and found Mrs. Penfield slowly fingering the spines of the books, looking for the right dates. She smiled when she saw Mary approach. "Well, your Bradley was always a looker," she said. "But so oblivious to the girls around him. I'm not surprised someone followed him home from the dance."

"Well, she's not very happy to discover he's married," she said. "So, we'd really like to discover who she is and see if we can help her move on."

"Hello, ladies," a male voice interrupted. "Can I be of any assistance?"

Mary turned to find Fred standing next to them. Mrs. Penfield sighed. "Fred, we don't need any help from you," she said firmly.

"Aren't you going to introduce me to your friend?" Fred asked, sending Mary a charming smile.

Mrs. Penfield rolled her eyes. "Fredrick Townsend, this is Mary Alden of Freeport, Illinois," she replied.

"Shhhhh," came a whispered order from the corner of the room. They all turned, and Mary saw another ghost, a trim, petite woman dressed in a long, black skirt and white blouse with a set of tiny eyeglasses perched on the tip of her nose. Her arms were crossed over her chest, and she was giving the entire group a disapproving glare.

"That's Miss Flora," Mrs. Penfield whispered. "She was one of our first librarians, and she doesn't like any noise in the building."

"I see," Mary whispered back. She turned to Miss Flora. "I apologize," she said softly. "I will be sure to keep my voice low."

With a disgusted sniff, Miss Flora glided away across the floor and melted into the wall.

"Good, she's going into the library," Fred said. "She'll find quite a bit to sniff and glare at in there."

"Now, Fred, we have work to do," Mrs. Penfield said, speaking to him as one would a small boy. "You go occupy yourself with something else."

He sighed, looked around and then smiled. "Sue looks bored," he said with a grin. "I'll see what I can do to liven her day."

He glided away and slipped behind the counter, upsetting the paper clip holder and upended the stapler. Then he turned to Mary and Mrs. Penfield and winked.

"He is quite the character," Mary said.

Mrs. Penfield sighed. "Yes, he is," she said. "He's a rascal. But a charming one. Now, let's start with the year Bradley graduated."

Mrs. Penfield started to pull out a book, but when Mary caught the glance of someone staring wide-eyed at a book levitating out of the shelf by itself, she quickly grabbed hold of the book, too.

"I can handle the weight," Mrs. Penfield gently scolded her.

"Yes, but I'm not sure the other patrons understand floating books," Mary whispered back.

A delighted laugh floated up from the old teacher. She shook her head. "You know, I quite forgot that I was dead," she chuckled. "Yes, of course, you should do the lifting while there are patrons about."

Chapter Seventeen

Mary sat at a small table in the corner of the Joiner Room with a stack of yearbooks next to her. She flipped the last page of the book that was dated three years after Bradley's graduation. She had reasoned that the ghost could have been a freshman when Bradley was a senior, so she needed to check those yearbooks. She also checked the yearbooks in the other directions. Perhaps the ghost was an older student who met Bradley when he was a freshman. But so far, after searching through nine yearbooks, no familiar face appeared.

Mary pulled out one book that she'd set to the side. It was Bradley's senior year, and she had found some fairly intriguing photos of him as the captain of the swim team. Opening the book to the page she'd bookmarked, she smiled at the photo of her husband in his youth. "You were a hunk then, and you're a hunk now," she whispered.

"Ah, appreciating the anatomy of the male species?" Mrs. Penfield asked, appearing next to her. Mary blushed.

"Well, I'm…" she paused.

Mrs. Penfield laughed. "Oh, don't be embarrassed," she said. "Your Mr. Alden was one of the best looking students we had at the high school."

Mary turned, surprised at the teacher's comment.

"What?" Mrs. Penfield asked with a smile. "Just because we were teachers doesn't mean we were blind. We never did anything inappropriate, but we also were grateful for the opportunity to see good-looking students." She winked at Mary. "There were enough of the other kind to keep us firmly grounded."

Mary chuckled softly. "I never thought of it that way," she said, and then she sighed. "I've looked through nine years of books, and I don't see her at all. This is so strange. They had to go to school together, didn't they? How else would she know him?"

"Well, perhaps her brother was on the swim team, and she went to the meets?" Mrs. Penfield suggested. "And perhaps one of Bradley's friends who wasn't on the team had a little sister who had a crush on him."

Nodding, Mary slid the final book back onto the pile. "You're right," she said. "This could be a long search." She lifted half the stack and carried them over to the shelf. "I'm having lunch with Bradley's friend Rick Thomas. Perhaps I'll ask him for some names of Bradley's friends."

Mrs. Penfield studied Mary for a moment. "Rick Thomas?" she questioned. "Really? Well, isn't that interesting."

After sliding the books into place, Mary turned to the old teacher. "Why do you say that?" she asked.

"Rick will be an interesting person for you to get to know," Mrs. Penfield said. "And I think you'll be good for him."

"I always worry when teachers tell me that something is going to be good for me," Mary replied with a smile. "That tends to mean there's going to be some hard work involved."

Mrs. Penfield chuckled and shook her head. "No, no hard work," she said. "Just a new way of looking at things."

"Did you find what you were looking for?" Sue asked, coming up behind Mary, her arms filled with the remainder of the books she'd left on the table.

"Oh, you didn't need to do that," Mary said as Sue slipped the books in place. "I was just cleaning up."

"I saw that," Sue replied. "And I just thought I'd help." She looked pointedly at Mary's belly. "You look like you have enough to carry."

Smiling, Mary nodded. "Actually, it's not that bad," she said. "But I appreciate your help."

"So, did you find what you were looking for?" Sue repeated.

"No, I'm afraid not," Mary replied. "I guess I'll need to come back and expand my search."

"Why don't you give me your contact information," Sue suggested, "just in case we run across something that will help?"

"Thank you," Mary replied, handing Sue a business card. "That would be wonderful."

Sue glanced around quickly and then lowered her voice. "You mentioned you see ghosts," she said. "Have you, er, seen anyone since you've been here?"

Nodding, Mary leaned toward Sue. "There have been three here," she said. "You know about

Fred, and he is quite a dapper gentleman and very friendly. Although, it seems he has a wicked sense of humor."

"Sounds just like him," Sue agreed.

"Then there's Miss Flora," Mary said.

Sue looked surprised. "Really? Miss Flora is here?" she asked, looking around.

"Well, she only stopped by for a moment to shush us," Mary said with a smile. "Then she moved on to the library. It sounds like you know about her."

"Miss Flora was the first librarian in Sycamore," Sue explained. "She actually troweled the cement onto the first brick that was laid for this building back in 1905. But she got sick and died before the building was completed."

"Well, it would make sense that she would want to be here," Mary said. "Wouldn't it?"

"It certainly would," Sue replied. "And the third?"

Mary looked past Sue to where Mrs. Penfield was standing and lifted her eyebrow in question. Mrs. Penfield cordially nodded, giving Mary permission. "The last ghost is Mrs. Penfield, a teacher from the high school," Mary said.

"I had Mrs. Penfield when I went to Sycamore High," Sue exclaimed, glancing around.

"She was my favorite teacher. It's so lovely that she's here. Does she like it here?"

"I love it here," Mrs. Penfield replied.

"She loves it here," Mary said.

Sue shook her head in wonder. "Thank you for coming by today," she said. "I'm afraid you've given us more answers than we've given you."

"Oh, I loved being here," Mary replied. "And I promise you I'll be back."

Chapter Eighteen

Mary met Rick at a fast food restaurant about three miles away from the library. It was famous for its Chicago-style hot dogs and Italian beef. Once seated, Rick looked across the table at Mary's meal, a Chicago-style hot dog, cheese fries and a chocolate shake, and shook his head.

"I'm so sorry," he said. "I should have suggested a healthier place."

Mary picked up the hot dog in both hands and looked over at him. "Are you kidding?" she asked incredulously. "This is a pregnant woman's dream come true." She brought the hot dog to her mouth and took a big bite. "Besides," she murmured as she chewed, "I can tell Bradley I had vegetables for lunch."

Rick chuckled. "Yes, I see vegetables all over that hot dog," he said skeptically.

"Excuse me?" Mary replied. "Tomatoes, cucumbers, peppers, celery salt…"

"Wait. You can't use celery salt as a vegetable," Rick argued.

"Why not?" Mary asked. "It came from a celery."

Rick nearly choked on his French fry. "I can see I'm not going to win this argument," he stated.

Mary grinned. "No, I've had months of practice," she said. "Let's see, potatoes and then there's all the beans."

"Beans?" he asked, looking confused.

Mary picked up her shake. "The chocolate comes for cocoa beans, and beans are a vegetable."

"You are amazing," he said. "But actually, beans are legumes."

Mary nodded. "Okay, I had vegetables, grains, dairy and legumes for lunch," she said easily as she dipped a fry into the cheese sauce. "How healthy am I?"

He sat back in his seat and stared at her for a moment. "Does Bradley have any idea what he's up against?" he asked a few moments later.

Her grin widened, and she nodded. "Oh yes," she said. "And he gave up a long time ago."

His smile turned into laughter, and it took him several moments before he was able to speak again. "Wow," he said, wiping his eyes. "I haven't laughed like that in a long time."

Mary studied the man sitting across from him. His skin had a pale pallor, and his eyes were shadowed. She could believe that he hadn't laughed, or even smiled in a long time. "Why?" she asked.

"Why what?" he replied, confused.

"Why haven't you laughed like that in a long time?" she asked, the laughter gone from her voice.

He picked up a narrow fry and tentatively dipped it in some ketchup. "I don't really know," he said. "I feel like it's been a long time since I've been able to be happy."

"Can you remember when it started?" Mary asked.

He chewed on the fry for a moment as he thought back and then looked at her. "I guess the last time I can remember being happy was at boot camp," he said. "I seemed to have changed when I went overseas."

"So, this is beginning to get really personal," Mary said, wondering why Mike had wanted her to speak with Rick, because this seemed like it was way out her league. "And you don't have to answer if you don't want to. But could it be PTSD?"

He sighed and picked up another fry. "You know, actually, I thought it could be," he said. "And I actually went in for counseling. But nothing. After a couple of years, even the counselors didn't know what to do with me."

He smiled sadly and shrugged. "I guess I just get to be sad."

Mary bent down to pick up another fry, but as she bent, out of the corner of her eye, she thought she saw something. Lifting her head, she studied Rick.

"What?" he asked.

Shaking her head, she smiled. "Sorry, I just thought I saw something," she replied and then shrugged. "But nothing's there."

"Funny you should say that," Rick said. "I'm always catching glimpses of things in mirrors or windows as I walk by." He wagged his eyebrows at her. "Like I'm being followed."

"So, you admit to being a spy," she replied in her best Russian accent.

He grinned. "I admit nothing," he said, imitating her accent.

"Well, admit it or not," she said, her voice serious again. "I'd really like to help you figure out what's going on."

"Are you a doctor or something?" Rick asked.

She shook her head. "No, just a friend," she said.

"I could actually use more of those," he said, his smile heartfelt. "Thank you."

"Don't thank me," Mary said. "I haven't done anything yet. But, I could use your help."

"Sure. Anything."

"Do you remember any of Bradley's friends who had sisters who might have had a crush on him?"

He sat back and nodded. "How much time do you have?"

Mary sighed dramatically and pulled a notepad out of her purse. "Okay, I'm ready," she said. "And I've got an extra pen just in case I run out of ink."

Chapter Nineteen

Mary arrived home a little before four p.m. and was surprised to find Bradley's cruiser parked in front of the house. She hurried from her car to the house and carefully opened the door, peeking into the house to avoid any jealous poltergeist or, at the very least, flying objects. "Is the coast clear?" she called out.

Bradley came walking out of the kitchen into the living room, wiping his hands on a dish towel. "Hey, welcome home," he said. "It looks like things are quiet so far."

Mary slipped into the house and closed the door behind her. "How was your day?" she asked, walking over to Bradley and lacing her arms around his neck.

"It's getting better," he replied, smiling down at her and then kissing her soundly. "Much better."

She grinned up at him. "You say the nicest things," she replied, "especially when you know that I had lunch with your best friend from high school and I have all kinds of dirt on you."

"Oh really?" he asked, cocking his head slightly to the side. "And what dirt is that?"

"Well, I have a *long* list of friends' siblings who were head-over-heels in love with you," she said.

He shook his head. "It couldn't be that long," he said. "I really was a dork in high school."

She looked up at him and saw that he really believed it. Stretching up, she kissed him and smiled. "You really are adorable," she said. She slipped out of his arms, took her coat off and hung it in the closet. She looked back at him over her shoulder. "By the way, Mrs. Penfield thought you were a hunk."

He thought about the comment for a moment. "I'm feeling a little uneasy about knowing that," he said. "Actually, the term would be creeped out."

Mary laughed. "And so you should be," she teased. "But she was very helpful at the Joiner Room."

"Did you have any luck?" he asked.

"No, I checked nine yearbooks, and our visitor is not in any of them," she replied. "So, I'll have to make another trip back there and see what I can find. How about you? Any luck with Eddie, the Koch's son?"

"Yeah, I..." he began, but stopped when the doorbell rang.

Bradley walked past Mary and opened the door. "Hi," he said. "Just in time."

Just in time, Mary wondered.

She didn't wonder long. Rosie, Stanley and Margo came into her home, each carrying a dish. "I asked Bradley if we could bring dinner over tonight," Rosie announced, walking past Mary to the kitchen. "And then we could discuss the case."

"Oh," Mary said, a little overwhelmed. "Well, that's nice."

"I made pot roast," Rosie said.

"And homemade Parker rolls," Stanley added.

"With chocolate cake," Margo said.

Mary felt an answering rumble in her stomach and smiled. "Wow. This is the way to work on a case."

A few minutes later, they were all seated around the kitchen table, and Bradley started to finish what he began to say to Mary. "I did a background check on their son," he said. "And, except for some financial issues, the guy's clean. He didn't even have an overdue parking ticket."

"How about the car?" Stanley asked as he liberally buttered a roll. "Did they find the brake cables had been tampered with?"

Bradley looked over at Stanley and sadly shook his head. "They didn't look," he said.

"What?" Stanley asked.

"The car was totaled in the accident," he explained. "And because of the age of the driver..."

"Because he was an old guy they figured he just drove off the road?" Stanley asked heatedly.

Nodding, Bradley continued. "Since they had no reason to suspect foul play, they just treated it like a car accident."

"So, if it were a murder, we have no evidence," Margo said.

Bradley shook his head. "No, I checked, and the car was crushed," he said. "So, no physical evidence."

"Well, there's always circumstantial evidence," Margo said with determination. "My daughter does a lot with circumstantial evidence. So, what's our next step?"

"I'd like to meet with Eddie," Mary said, "and just talk to him about his parents. Maybe get an idea of how he feels about their death."

"By the way," Bradley said, "he hasn't taken any of their money."

"What?" Stanley asked.

"He hasn't touched a cent of their estate," Bradley replied.

"Well, that's one way to throw them off the trail," Stanley grumbled.

"What trail?" Rosie asked. "Everyone thought it was an accident. There is no trail."

Stanley grumbled and bit the end off a roll. "Well, you can't be too careful iffen you're feeling like people are watching you."

Margo looked at Stanley, and Rosie and bit back a chuckle. "Well, while you speak with Eddie, we could talk to some of their friends and see if anyone else could be a suspect," she suggested.

Stanley hit his fist on the table, causing everyone to jump, and then chuckling he nodded. "That's exactly what we should be doing, hunting for other guilty parties," he said. "We could talk to some of my buddies at the VFW. They'd be able to help us put together a list."

"But we have to be careful," Margo inserted. "We can't give away too much. One of them might be the murderer."

Stanley looked aghast. "Not one of the guys at the VFW," he said. "I'd…"

"If you say you'd stake your life on it, Stanley Wagner, I'll…I'll…well, I don't know what I'll do,"

Rosie said. "You don't know any of those men except for meetings and dinners. You have no idea what they would do."

Stanley sighed. "Okay, we'll be sneaky-like," he said.

Margo smiled. "I love being sneaky," she said, scooping a little more potatoes and vegetables onto her plate. "It's actually one of my most favorite things to do."

Chapter Twenty

"I forgot to ask you," Bradley said later that evening as they were cleaning up the kitchen together. "How was your lunch with Rick?"

After their guests had left, they'd run over to the Brennans to visit with Clarissa for a little while and then had come home to clean things up. Mary handed Bradley a wet platter to dry and then reached into the sink and pulled out the drain, letting the water slowly escape. "He's a really nice guy," she said. "And he had a few great stories about you." She paused and leaned against the counter. "But there are a couple of things that really trouble me about him."

Bradley wiped the platter and then placed it up on one of the top shelves. "What?"

"Well, first, he said that he hadn't been happy in a long time," she said, shaking her head. "It was so sad. He couldn't even remember when it started. All he could remember was being happy in boot camp."

Nodding, Bradley took his damp dishtowel and hung it over the rack next to the sink. "I remember him in boot camp," he said. "Don't get me wrong. It was hard, but somehow Rick made it a lot easier for the rest of us. His personality, his joking, made it bearable."

"So did you notice a change in him?" Mary asked.

He thought about his answer for a minute. "Yeah, I guess after we'd served overseas, things seemed different," he said. "I mean, I don't think we really understood what was going to happen when we went to war. You think when you're young that it's all glory, that there's a definite right and wrong, black and white—no gray areas. But when you get over there, you realize that it's dirty, messy, exhausting, unfair and the furthest thing from what you'd imagined it to be. It kind of changes everyone."

"But with Rick it was different?" she prompted.

He nodded slowly. "Yeah. Yeah, now that I think about it, it was different with him," he replied. "I wonder if he has PTSD."

"I asked him about that," she admitted.

He smiled at her. "Well, of course you did," he said.

She shrugged, a little embarrassed. "Well, Mike said this was important," she defended. "So, I wanted to make sure I got all the information."

"Information on what?" Mike asked, appearing next to them.

"Thanks. Information on Rick," Mary said. "I had lunch with him today."

"Good," Mike replied. "By the way, Clarissa is finally settled down with Maggie and considering sleeping."

Bradley laughed. "I don't know where they get the energy," he said. "Mary was saying that Rick told her he hadn't been happy since boot camp, and I wondered if he had PTSD."

"He told me that he considered it, too," Mary added. "And he even went to see some counselors. But they couldn't help him. He was still sad."

Bradley nodded. "It was like he carried around a shadow."

Mary quickly looked over at him. "What did you say?" she asked.

"Like he carried around this shadow?"

"Yeah, that," she said. "When I was at lunch with him, for a moment I thought there was someone, something, right behind him. But then it was gone. I figured I must have imagined it."

"You tend to have pretty good instincts when it comes to things like that," Bradley said.

"And then Rick told me that he often thought he was seeing things out of the corner of his eye," she continued. "Especially when he was walking past a mirror or a window."

"Do spirits attach themselves to humans?" Bradley asked Mike.

Mike shrugged. "I don't know for sure," he said. "But it makes sense, doesn't it? When you talk about possession, it's just a spirit attaching itself to someone."

"But could they, not totally possess, just influence them?" Mary asked.

"That's a good question," Mike replied. "And something I'm going to have to do a little research on."

"I wonder if Rick were put under hypnosis," Mary said.

Bradley smiled. "Ian could probably meet us in Sycamore," he added.

"We could introduce him to Chicago-style hot dogs," Mary said with a grin.

"I'll call him in the morning," Bradley said.

Chapter Twenty-one

Bradley stood on the top step on the second floor, a flashlight clutched in his hand, listening to the sounds below. They were subtle sounds: a cabinet opening and closing, movement across the floor, a drawer opening. But it was enough to know there was someone downstairs in their home. Was it human or specter? The only way to know was to investigate. He cautiously slipped one foot on the next step, making sure to place his foot near the side of the stair where the supports underneath the step stopped any creaking. Slowly, step by step, he moved downstairs, the flashlight dimmed against his palm.

Reaching the first floor, he glanced at the door—still locked from the inside. Obviously it wasn't the point of entry. He listened and heard soft noises coming from the kitchen. The intruder was still in his home. Pressing himself against the living room wall, he sidled towards the kitchen, hoping to catch the invader unaware. He paused for a moment at the closet door, wondering if he should retrieve his gun. Deciding that the noise from the opening door would alert whoever it was in the kitchen, he decided that surprise was his best weapon.

With the stealth of a jungle cat, he crept the remaining few feet to the entrance of the kitchen, jumped around shining the flashlight into the room and screamed, "Freeze!" It took a few seconds for his eyes to adjust to the light and discern what he'd caught. In the beam of the flashlight, a pair of eyes, widened in surprise, stared back at him. With a fork filled with chocolate cake halfway between the plate on the counter and her mouth, Mary stood frozen in place.

"Mary?" Bradley asked, dropping the flashlight and turning on the kitchen light. "Why are you down here eating in the dark?"

She swallowed loudly and then took a deep breath, trying to get her heart to resume a normal pace. "Because I was hungry," she replied, her voice a little shaky. "And when you stand up and eat, it's fewer calories."

"Oh, sweetheart," he said, coming around and enveloping her in his arms. "I am so sorry I scared you." Mary's tummy jumped.

"Hiccup."

He stepped away from her. "What was that?"

"Hiccup. Hiccup. Hiccup."

Mary put her hands on her stomach and her eyes widened in amazement. "The baby has the hiccups," she said softly. "How sweet is that?"

Bradley placed his hand on her belly. "Hiccup. Hiccup. Hiccup. Hiccup."

"That's amazing," he said. "I didn't know they had hiccups inside you."

She looked back at him. "Well, maybe it has something to do with his mother being scared to death by father," she suggested.

"I really do apologize," he said. "I thought someone had broken in."

"To eat our cake?" she asked.

He smiled down at her. "Well, it is Rosie's chocolate cake," he reasoned.

She smiled. "That's true," she said. "Point taken."

"Hiccup. Hiccup. Hiccup."

"Oh, poor thing," Mary said. "I hope it doesn't hurt."

"Well, I could…" Bradley began.

"If you are even thinking about scaring us again, you can forget it," she said.

He chuckled. "Okay, it's forgotten. Maybe if you drink a lot of water."

"And then I'll be up all night going to the bathroom," she reminded him.

Sighing, he reached up over her and pulled a plate out of the cabinet. "Any more of that cake left?" he asked.

She grinned and nodded. "In the fridge," she said, picking up her own plate and carrying it to the table.

Bradley walked over to the fridge and pulled out the plate of cake. Then he turned to Mary. "Glass of milk?" he asked.

"That would be lovely," she replied.

"Hiccup. Hiccup. Hiccup."

"Okay, this is kind of adorable," she said.

"Yeah, it really is," Bradley said as he put the milk on the counter and searched for two cups.

An hour later Mary lay in her bed, surrounded by pillows, her hands resting on her belly. "Hiccup. Hiccup. Hiccup."

She groaned and looked at the bedside clock that read 1:00 AM. "Oh, yeah, adorable," she grumbled. "Remind me to ground you once you're born."

Chapter Twenty-two

The Nine East café was crowded with the usual, early morning, coffee throng, but somehow Mary was able to pick Eddie Koch out of the crowd right away. He was a middle-aged man who looked more like his mother than his father, and he was sitting morosely at a corner table, sipping from a tall mug of coffee. Mary smiled at Brenda as she passed the crowded counter.

"Hey, how are you feeling?" Brenda called.

"Like I'm ready to have this baby," Mary replied.

Brenda laughed. "So how much longer?"

"Another two months," Mary said.

Shaking her head sympathetically, Brenda smiled. "Oh, honey, you don't even know uncomfortable yet," she said.

"Thanks for the pep talk," Mary said, rolling her eyes.

Laughing in response, Brenda shrugged. "It is what it is," she said. "So, what can I get you?"

"Do you have any herb teas with ginger?" Mary asked.

"Upset stomach?" Brenda asked.

Looking a little chagrined, Mary nodded. "Chocolate cake at midnight."

"Rosie's cake?" Brenda asked.

Mary nodded.

"Well, then I can hardly blame you," Brenda said. "I've got something that will be perfect. Take a seat and I'll find you."

Mary walked over to Eddie and extended her hand. "Hi, I'm Mary," she said. "Thanks for meeting with me."

Eddie looked up and couldn't hide his surprise when he saw Mary's shape. When she struggled a little to get up on the tall chair, he immediately slid off his seat to help her. "Would you like to sit somewhere else?" he asked, concern in his voice. "Like a booth or one of the couches?"

Mary shook her head and smiled at him. "No, actually, once I'm up here, I'm good."

He eyed her suspiciously. "Are you sure?"

"Yes, really," she replied. "I'm fine."

He got back on his chair and turned to her. "You said you wanted to talk to me about my parents," he said. "I don't understand."

"I'm a private investigator," she said. "And I've been hired to investigate your parents' deaths."

He shook his head, confused. "Wait. What? They died in a car accident," he said. "It was months ago. Why is someone investigating things now?"

"Well, new information has come forward that could indicate that perhaps it wasn't just a car accident," she said.

"Are you telling me that someone killed my mom and dad?" he asked. Then, his eyes widening, he stared at her for a moment. "Do you think I killed my parents?"

"Is there any reason I should think that?" she asked.

Angrily shaking his head, he pushed back against the table, his chair scraping on the floor. "I don't have to take this crap," he said, sliding off the chair. "I'm leaving."

He walked around Mary towards the door. "Wait," Mary called, sliding around in the chair. She caught the edge of the chair with her rib and winced in pain. "Ouch," she cried out.

Eddie stopped and immediately came back to her. "Are you okay?" he asked.

She took a deep breath and nodded slowly. "I forget that I'm not as small as I used to be," she said.

She looked at him. "Could you…could we…just talk for a few moments?"

With a sigh, he nodded and went back to his chair. "I apologize," he said. "I just…" His voice broke. "I just miss them."

"I can't imagine how it would be to lose your parents at the same time," Mary said softly. "I think I would be devastated."

"I had an argument with my dad," he confessed. "He and Mom were at my house, and I asked him for a loan. He turned me down, and we argued." He paused and took a deep breath. "It was so stupid. He was totally right. I was an idiot. And I never got to tell him that I was sorry."

Frasier and Shirley appeared at the table next to them, Shirley dabbing at her eyes.

"See, I told you," Shirley said to Frasier.

"I can't believe it took me dying to get him to say I was right," Frasier replied.

"I'm sure they know you're sorry," Mary said.

"You can't know that," Eddie argued.

Mary shrugged. "Well, actually, you'd be surprised," she replied quietly and then added. "So what happened that night?"

He ran his hand over his face, dashing away the errant tears, and took a deep breath. "I lost my job and I was tired of working for other people," he said. "So I wanted to start my own business. I asked Dad for the front money and he refused. He told me that if I wanted to start my own business, I needed to work for it. I needed to start small and then expand, not have a turn-key operation right away."

"That must have been disappointing," Mary replied. "It sounds like you were counting on him."

He nodded. "I was," he said. "I had this big plan. I was going to be the boss. I was going to show my old boss and my friends that I could do it without them."

"And then he turned you down," Mary said.

"Yeah, I was so mad," Eddie admitted. "I didn't want to start from the bottom. I knew he had the money. I thought he was being selfish."

"So, what happened?"

"I told them to leave," he said, tears filling his eyes. "I told them if they couldn't help me when I needed them, what the hell kind of parents were they."

"We knew he was just disappointed," Shirley said. "Children say unkind things all the time they don't really mean."

"They left," he said, sniffling back the tears. "And then the police came to the door a couple hours later telling me they were both dead."

He looked up at the ceiling for a moment, trying to gain control of his emotions. "It was like I killed them," he said. "If I hadn't sent them away, if they hadn't been upset, if I'd only…"

Mary reached over and put her hand on Eddie's hand. "No, you can't play the what if game," she said. "You'll drive yourself crazy."

He nodded. "Well, actually, I nearly did," he said. "I took Dad's words to heart. I started my business from the bottom. I didn't touch any of his money. I've been working sixteen hour days, and you know what? He was right. I feel like I've finally done something with my life." He cradled his head in his hand. "He was right."

"Damn, he did listen," Frasier said, with a proud smile on his face. "That's my boy."

"I'm sure your parents would be very proud of you," Mary said.

He lifted his head and turned to her. "Well, I'm doing everything in my power to see that they have cause to be," he said. He studied Mary for a moment. "If you really believe that my parents' death was not an accident, I would like to help in any way I can."

"Thank you," Mary said, glancing over at Shirley and Frasier. "I think you've already helped me more than you know. But I promise I'll keep you informed."

He slid out of the chair and offered her his hand. "Thank you," he said, and then he paused. "You know, it's almost like I can feel them here with us now. Thank you. It's been very comforting to speak with you."

"You're welcome," Mary replied. "Please call me if you think of anything or need anything."

"Thanks, I will."

Chapter Twenty-three

The restaurant on Galena Avenue advertised with large letters on their plate glass windows a Senior's Menu, and the senior citizens of the Freeport area took full advantage of it. Their parking lot filled with older model, well cared for sedans, and the waitresses were used to the sometimes odd requests from their aging customers.

Stanley, Rosie and Margo sat at a corner table looking at the menu. "I don't know why you insist on coming here?" Rosie whispered behind her menu. "It's obvious that both Margo and I are too young to participate in the senior discount."

Stanley looked over at his wife, and seeing the look in her eye, thought a moment before answering. "What do you mean?" he grumbled in his usual way. "Don't the discount start at fifty?"

A soft smile spread across her face, and she nodded happily. "No, it doesn't," she replied.

"Oh, well, I'll just use the discount, and you and Margo will have to order off the regular menu," he said, and then he smiled at her. "It's nice for an old guy like me to have two young lookers join him for breakfast."

"You are such a charmer," Rosie replied, leaning over and kissing his wrinkled cheek.

"Stanley, I can honestly say that you are the best thing that ever happened to Rosie," Margo added. "She's a lucky gal."

Stanley reached over and put his hand over Rosie's hand. "No, Margo, I'm the lucky one," he said, his eyes still filled with newlywed love. "And I thank my lucky stars every day."

"Stanley. Stanley, is that you over there?" a male voice called out from the front of the restaurant.

Annoyed, Stanley sighed. "Melvin always likes to make an entrance," he said, raising his hand and motioning the man over to their table. "He's a little annoying, but he knows everyone at the VFW and he and Frasier were best friends."

"Well, we can put up with just about anything to get good information," Margo whispered, leaning forward. "Besides, he's probably not as bad as you think."

Melvin Redman made his way slowly to the table, stopping and chatting with most of the other patrons in the restaurant. He stopped at their table, grabbed Rosie's hand and kissed it. "Too bad Stanley found you first, Rosie," he said with an exaggerated sigh. "We could have made such beautiful music together."

Margo looked across the table and shook her head. "Okay, I admit it," she said, biting back a smile. "I was wrong."

Melvin turned to Margo and wiggled his eyebrows. "Why hello lovely lady," he said, dropping Rosie's hand with a thump. "I don't believe we've been introduced."

Margo rolled her eyes and shook her head. "You're right," she said shortly. "We haven't."

She turned her attention back to the menu, ignoring the man standing beside her. Slightly flustered, Melvin pulled up a seat and picked up his own menu. "So, Stanley," he said, "other than these ladies, what looks good today?"

The waitress chose that moment to come to their table. "Hi, have you decided what you'd like?" she asked.

"I'd like a million dollars," Melvin said, chuckling at himself.

The waitress pasted on a tired smile and nodded. "I meant on the menu," she said.

"Well, I know that," Melvin laughed. "I was just trying to brighten your day."

"Well, thank you," the waitress replied. "And what would you like to order?"

"Why don't we place our orders first?" Margo suggested before Melvin could say another word. "And that will give Melvin a moment to review the menu."

Subdued by Margo's tone, Melvin buried his head in the menu and then, when it was his turn, ordered in a concise and straightforward manner.

"I think I need to apologize," he said to the group. "I tend to go overboard when I'm trying to impress people. I think I got carried away."

Margo turned and smiled at him. "Well, that was very nicely done," she said. "I'm Margo. It's nice to meet you."

"Thank you, Margo," he said. "Now Stanley, you mentioned you wanted to speak to me about something."

Stanley nodded. "Yes, Margo here has some friends in the Freeport area she lost touch with," Stanley said. "And she hasn't been able to reach them. I told her you knew just about everyone in this town and you might be able to help."

Taking her cue from Stanley, Margo nodded. "Yes, I'm wondering if perhaps they've moved," she said. "I have to admit that I'm a little worried."

"Oh? Who are they?" Melvin asked.

"Shirley and Frasier Koch," Margo said.

Melvin's face dropped. "Oh, I'm so sorry," he said. "But they both passed away several months ago."

Margo's shocked face even impressed Rosie and Stanley. "No, they were both so healthy," she said.

"Well, it was a car accident," Melvin said. "Looked like Frasier was driving a little too fast for conditions." He shook his head. "It was a quite a tragedy."

"So, they're sure it was an accident?" Margo asked.

Melvin paused and then glanced around the room. Leaning forward, he lowered his voice. "If you ask me, I'd say there was more to it," he said. "Frasier drove those roads all the time."

"Really?" Margo asked. "What do you think happened?"

"I think his son had something to do with it," he said. "That kid was always out of money. I could see him tampering with his parents' car."

"Their own son?" Margo asked. "Did the police investigate?"

"No," Melvin replied, sitting back in his chair. "And why would they? Just an elderly couple and a car accident. Happens all the time."

Chapter Twenty-four

The midday sun was shining down on the front porch when Mary pulled up in front of her house. Bradley was at the police station, and Clarissa was at school. So this was the perfect time, Mary reasoned, to have a heart to heart with their adolescent ghost.

Opening the front door, she stepped inside, closed the door behind and waited. She could hear the soft clicks coming from the grandfather clock in the hall, the subtle whoosh as the furnace started another cycle and the hum of the refrigerator. Normal sounds. Comforting sounds. Familiar sounds.

Slipping her coat off, she laid it on a nearby chair and slowly walked through the living room. "Hello?" she called out tentatively. "Hello. I just want to talk to you."

"Yeah, sure, we can talk."

The male voice made Mary jump, and she spun around to see Frasier and Shirley sitting on the couch behind her. Shirley slapped Frasier's arm. "I told you she wasn't talking to us," she scolded. "And I told you we should have used the front door. We scared her nearly to death."

"All these rules," Frasier complained. "I'm dead, okay? I don't get all the rules."

He looked up at Mary. "I'm really sorry," he said. "I didn't mean to scare you."

She took a deep breath and smiled. "You did startle me," she confessed. "But, I've been a little more on edge lately, so it wasn't all your fault."

Looking around the otherwise empty house, she shrugged and sat down on the chair across from the couch. "I was really impressed with your son," she said.

Shirley smiled. "He's always been such a good boy," she said.

"He's a man, Shirl," Frasier said. "And we still don't know for sure that he didn't do it."

"You have always been blind to what's right in front of your face," Shirley replied, turning to face her husband. "Eddie is in grief. Eddie is doing his best to live the kind of life he thinks you would want him to lead. Can't you for once in your life give him a little credit?"

"I can't," Frasier replied.

"What?" Shirley asked, incredulous.

"I can't for once in my life," Frasier repeated sarcastically. "Because I'm dead, Shirl. Get it?"

She slapped his arm again. "This is not the time to be funny," she said shortly. "You need to really look at your son and see what he's accomplished. Stop looking at what he hasn't done and look at what he has."

He sighed softly and nodded. "I really want to believe that he wouldn't do this," he said. "But Shirl, we're dead. If he didn't do it, then who did?"

"That's my job," Mary said. "And I will find out who's responsible. Just be patient with me for a little while."

Frasier shrugged. "I thought we were being patient," he said. "You were the one who called us."

Mary shook her head. "Well, actually, I was trying to get in contact with someone else. Someone who's not as patient with me as you both are."

"Oh, I'm so sorry," Shirley replied, standing up and pulling on Frasier. "We just barged in, thinking it was us. Come on Frasier, we need to let Mary get her work done."

"No, really, I'm glad we spoke," Mary said. "And if you can think of anyone else who might have…" She paused, not sure how she wanted to phrase things.

"Wanted us dead?" Frasier inserted, his voice low. "Well, that's something you don't think about every day."

126

Frasier stood and put his arm around his wife. He shook his head sadly. "If anyone wanted to kill us," he said to her, "it would have been because of me, not you. I'm so sorry I took you down with me."

She leaned her head on his shoulder. "Oh, Fray," she said. "I wouldn't have wanted to live without you."

He hugged her quickly and then turned to Mary. "So, what should we be looking for?" he asked.

"Well, most murders are committed for some really basic reasons: money, power, love or to cover up another crime," she said. "So, we've covered the money aspect. Now think about those other ones."

Frasier shook his head. "We can think about them," he said. "But I know they don't apply. Hell, the only power I had was vice-chair of the VFW."

Shirley smiled up at him. "But you were going to be president," she said. "Everyone loved you there."

He blushed slightly and then looked over to Mary. "We'll think about it," he promised. "And then we'll get back to you."

He looked down at his wife. "Ready Shirl?"

She smiled up at him. "Ready."

They slowly faded away, still smiling at each other. Mary sighed and leaned back in her chair, lifting her feet and propping them on top of the ottoman.

"That was sweet," Mike said as he faded into view, sitting on the couch.

Mary nodded. "Yes, it really was," she said. "And my gut tells me Eddie isn't the killer."

"Are you sure your gut isn't so filled with motherly instincts that you don't want to see something that's there?" he asked.

"No," she said simply. "I trust my instincts, even my pregnant instincts." She paused and studied him for a moment. "Unless there's something you know that you're not telling me."

He smiled and shook his head. "No. Nothing. Nothing at all," he said. "Just testing."

"Testing?" she asked, her eyes narrowing at the thought. She slipped her feet off the ottoman and leaned forward. "You really think you ought to be testing me in my frame of mind?"

His smile faltered, and he stepped backwards. "I meant, um, brainstorming," he stuttered. "Not testing. Never testing." He glanced around the room. "Who said that word? Not me."

Grinning at him, she leaned back in her chair, put her feet back on the ottoman and nodded. "Better. Much better," she said. "So, what's up?"

"I haven't been able to have a conversation with our high school sweetheart," he said. "I've tried, but she's not in the mood to talk."

"That's so strange," Mary said. "Why won't she let us help her? There's obviously something that's keeping her here."

"Maybe she doesn't want to go," Mike suggested. "But I don't get it."

Mary sighed. "I do," she said. "A girl's first crush is a hard one to get over. And she really never forgets him. She's still in love with Bradley."

Mike leaned back on the couch, propped his feet up next to Mary's and laced his hands behind his head. "So, how do you feel about having another woman around the house for the rest of your life?" he teased.

Mary picked up a pillow and threw it in his direction. It flew through him and landed on the corner of the couch. "Mike," she said.

"Yes?" he asked.

"Shut up."

Chapter Twenty-five

Eddie Koch locked up his business during his lunch hour and hurried to his car. It was nearly noon, and he didn't have much time before he had to be back on the job. He pulled down the street and headed towards the outskirts of town.

By chance, Bradley had been on his way across town when he saw Eddie hurry to his car. He'd seen his photo when he ran the background check on him. Bradley had thought he looked like a nice guy. But, now there was something about the way he carried himself, like he was trying to hide something, that caught Bradley's eye. He picked up the radio.

"Hey Dorothy, it's Bradley," he said. "I've got a lead on a case I'm working on, and I'm following a suspect out of town. I'll keep you informed."

"Do you want backup?" Dorothy asked.

"No, I think I want to keep this one on the downlow," Bradley said. "But I'll turn the tracker on, in case you don't hear from me for a while."

"Okay, be safe out there," Dorothy said.

"Thanks, I will," he replied.

Eddie's car twisted north through downtown and then headed out on Highway 75. Bradley kept far enough behind him so he could keep an eye on him but not look like he was trailing him. Finally, Eddie turned into a long driveway that headed toward the large junkyard on Henderson Road. Bradley passed the main gate and took a secondary road that led to the back of the property. He'd have a better view from there.

Bradley pulled the cruiser up on the hill behind the junkyard just in time to see Eddie pull up in front of the main building. He climbed out of his car and hurried through the door. A moment later Eddie, with the owner of the junkyard, walked across the lot towards another area that was gated off from the rest. The owner pulled a keychain from his waistband and opened the padlock that secured the gate. Pulling the gate wide, both men walked inside to an older model car that had obviously been in an accident.

Bradley pulled some binoculars out of the cruiser and focused in on the car. It was the same make and model as the car Frasier Koch had been driving when he got into the accident. "I thought they destroyed that months ago," Bradley said to himself.

He watched as Eddie pulled his wallet out of his back pocket and handed the junkyard owner several bills. The owner counted the money and then shook Eddie's hand. The owner went back to the office and left Eddie with the car.

Through the lens, Bradley could see Eddie yanking open the car door and climbing in. For several minutes Eddie was inside the car until finally he came out, holding something in his hand. Eddie walked through the gate and then stopped and spoke with the owner once again.

A few moments later, Eddie got in his car and drove away.

Bradley waited until he gave Eddie enough time to drive away before he went down to the main building.

"Hey, Chief," Gregg Alber, the owner of the yard said. "What's up?"

"I just noticed that Eddie Koch stopped by," Bradley replied. "What was that all about?"

Gregg hesitated for a moment and then shrugged. "Can you keep a secret?"

"You do realize who you're talking to," Bradley replied.

Gregg smiled. "Yeah, I do and it's not that kind of secret," he said. "Really, it's not a big deal."

"Okay. Yeah, I can keep a secret if it's not that kind of secret," Bradley said.

"Well, the insurance company paid us to crush the car," Gregg said. "But Eddie wasn't ready

132

to see it go. It was like his last connection to his parents. So, he asked me to hold on to it for a while."

Bradley nodded. "That was nice of you."

"Hey, I got the space," Gregg said. "And I really feel for the guy."

"So, why the visit?" Bradley asked.

Gregg shrugged again. "I guess he's ready now," he said. "Told me to go ahead and crush it. Actually, he said the sooner the better. Weird, right?"

Bradley nodded. "Yeah, weird. Hey, if you don't mind, could you not destroy the car until I get back to you? And maybe keep it just between the two of us."

Gregg studied Bradley for a moment and nodded with understanding. "You bet, Chief. Like I said, I got plenty of room," he replied. "Have a good afternoon."

"Yeah, you too."

Chapter Twenty-six

The VFW weekly luncheon was held at the Freeport Armory. Long tables were set out on the floor of the large meeting room, wrapped in white tablecloth paper and adorned with small centerpieces of half-circles of Styrofoam painted either red, white or blue and small American flags on dowels stuck into them.

Stanley led the way to a table in the middle of the room. "Iffen we sit here, we can hear conversations all around us," he said.

Margo shook her head. "At the next table?" she asked, skeptically.

Rosie smiled and nodded. "Most of the men here are going deaf, and they refuse to admit it," she said. "So everyone shouts everything. It's very easy to eavesdrop on several conversations." She grinned. "Actually, that's what keeps me coming back every week. The things you hear will shock you."

Chuckling, Margo took her seat in the metal folding chair next to Rosie and across the table from Stanley. "Well, this ought to be interesting, if nothing else," she said.

Dozens of people filed into the room, some by themselves and others as couples, taking their places at the table. Most greeted Stanley and Rosie warmly and welcomed Margo eagerly. A few minutes after they were seated, Melvin hurried over to the table, placed his coat over the chair next to Stanley's and smiled at the ladies. "I've got news for you," he said. "But my responsibilities come first." He rolled his eyes in mock weariness. "A president's job is never done."

After he hurried away, Margo turned to Rosie. "He's the president?" she whispered. "I have to admit that I'm a little surprised."

Rosie leaned towards her friend. "Well, although he has an odd sense of humor, he does seem to enjoy doing volunteer work," she replied softly.

"I guess it takes all kinds," Margo said, shaking her head.

Rosie chuckled softly. "Yes, it does."

"Ladies and gentlemen," Melvin's voice boomed out over the screechy P.A. system. "Welcome to the Freeport VFW luncheon. We'd like to welcome any visitors who are with us today and hope you enjoy yourself."

An elderly man in a walker made his way slowly up the aisles between the tables. He pulled out the chair on the other side of Margo and sat down.

"Howdy," he said loudly, his voice echoing throughout the room. "You a visitor?"

Margo nodded and smiled.

"Now for the announcements," Melvin said.

"What's your name?" the old man shouted, drowning out Melvin.

Embarrassed, Margo turned to him with a finger over her lips. "Shhhh," she pleaded.

"What's that you say?" the old man asked. "I couldn't hear you."

Desperate, she turned to him. "Margo," she whispered quickly. "My name is Margo."

He smiled. "Margaret," he said. "My late wife's name was Margaret."

Rosie leaned towards Margo and whispered in her ear. "No, it wasn't," she said. "It was Lois."

Margo nearly snorted. "Nice to meet you," she whispered.

"Can't hear you," the old man shouted. "Melvin's making too much noise. Give some people a microphone and they think they can talk over everything."

"If it's all right with Butch, we will now stand and sing our national anthem and say the Pledge of Allegiance," Melvin said from the front of the room.

Butch smiled and winked at Margo. "I get to him every time," he cackled as he pulled himself up to stand. "Man's too big for his britches."

The room proceeded with the opening, and in a few minutes they were seated once again. "I'll offer grace over the food," Melvin announced.

"We used to have a preacher come in and do that," Butch stated emphatically. "But I guess Melvin figures he's closer to God than any of them."

Stifling a chuckle, Margo bowed her head with the rest of the group and listened to Melvin's prayer. When it finally ended, Butch looked up and shook his head. "Food's getting cold with all this talking," he complained. "Why don't you sit down and let us enjoy our lunch?"

His face red, Melvin placed the microphone on the podium and marched back to their table. "Butch" he said curtly, acknowledging the man with a nod.

"Mel," Butch replied with a cackle. "Have you met Margaret?"

"Margo," Margo corrected him.

"She's from…" Butch turned to her. "Where did you say you were from?"

"Deadwood," she replied.

"Where the hell is that?" he asked.

"In South Dakota," Margo replied. "Near Mount Rushmore."

Their conversation was interrupted by the arrival of their salad plates. After the plate had been placed in front of her, Margo turned to Rosie. "Well, this is impressive," she said. "I thought it would be buffet style."

Pouring her dressing over the cut lettuce, Rosie smiled. "Well, with all the canes and walkers, we decided it would be safer and quicker if we just hired the caterer to serve," she said.

Margo chuckled. "Good idea."

Melvin leaned forward in his chair and put a piece of paper in the middle of the table. "I spent the morning compiling a list of people I thought might be responsible for the…" He turned and gazed at Butch who was unabashedly listening to their conversation. "The you-know-what."

"You got secrets?" Butch asked. "I always enjoy a good secret."

"Maybe we should discuss this later," Rosie suggested.

Melvin slid the paper over to Margo. "Why don't you look it over, and then maybe you and I could meet together?" he said, an eager glint in his eye.

Margo took the paper and nodded. "Thank you, Melvin," she said. "I'll look it over and get back to you."

"Make sure you bring enough money to pay your own way," Butch inserted. "Mel's known for being on the cheap side."

Lowering her head to hide her smile, Margo missed the look that passed between the two men. And had she seen it, she might have had a totally different idea about the investigation.

Chapter Twenty-seven

Mary slowly opened her eyes. She didn't know where she was or, actually, what day of the week it was. She stared at the material in front of her for a moment, squinting her eyes to bring it into focus. She finally recognized it. It was the back of the couch. She must have fallen asleep on the couch. She slowly rolled over and discovered there was an afghan tucked around her.

"Did I wake you up?" Bradley asked, sitting across from her. "I'm so sorry."

She stretched and then shook her head. "No. I just woke up on my own," she said. "How long have I been sleeping?"

"Well, you were crashed out when I got home about an hour ago," he said. "That's when I tucked you in. And it's nearly three."

Her eyes popped open. "Are you kidding?" she asked. "Nearly three? I sat down at one. I've been asleep for two hours."

He smiled at her. "You must have needed it," he said.

"I actually do feel pretty great," she admitted, sitting up and stretching again. She paused. "And I'm starving."

Laughing, Bradley stood up and helped Mary off the couch. "Well, I'm sure we can find something for lunch," he said. "What sounds good?"

"Chocolate cake?" she asked with a grin.

He shook his head. "Real food first," he said. "Then dessert."

She paused, looked down at her belly and then looked up at him. "Do I look like an elephant?" she asked.

Bradley smiled down at Mary and shook his head. "No, you don't look like an elephant," he said. "Why would you think that?"

She shrugged. "I don't know. Something I read somewhere," she said with a sigh. "It just feels like I've been pregnant forever."

He pulled her into his arms and hugged her. "You are perfect," he said. "You are adorable. And I think you are still the most beautiful woman in the world."

She laid her head against his chest and sighed happily. "Thank you," she said. "I needed that."

He slipped his arm around her shoulders and led her across the room to the kitchen. "So, how was your day?" he asked.

"Good," she said, leaning against him. "I spoke with Eddie, Shirley's and Frasier's son. I spoke with Shirley and Frasier. And I didn't get attacked by a poltergeist when I came home."

"Wow, sounds like a winner," Bradley said with a smile. "What did you think of Eddie?"

She walked over to the cupboards and pulled out a few plates. "I liked him," she said. "And I find it hard to believe he murdered his parents."

Bradley opened the refrigerator and pulled out a container of sliced roast beef and some cheese. "So, does that mean you're ruling him out?" he asked as he balanced lettuce, pickles and mayonnaise in his arms.

Crossing over to help him, Mary shook her head as she grabbed the lettuce and pickle jar. "No," she said, placing the items on the counter. "I need more information before I do that."

"Okay, I might have a little more information for you," he said. "I saw Eddie at the junkyard this afternoon."

She opened the pickle jar, pulled out a spear and bit into it. "At the junkyard?" she asked.

"You need some ice cream with that?" Bradley asked with a grin.

She wrinkled her nose at him. "Very funny," she said, taking another bite. "No. I don't want ice cream." And then she smiled. "I want chocolate cake."

"With pickles?" he asked. "That's gross."

She grinned. "Yes. Yes it is," she said. "So, what was Eddie doing at the junk yard?"

"Well, it turns out the Koch's car didn't get destroyed," he said. "Gregg's been keeping it at the junkyard in a fenced off area, out of sight. Eddie stopped by this afternoon to ask Gregg to crush it. The sooner the better."

"Crap," Mary said with a sigh. "I really liked him. He totally snookered me."

Bradley shrugged. "Well, we don't know anything yet," he said. "But let's keep him on the top of our suspects list."

Mary bit down on her pickle spear. "Yeah, good idea."

A few minutes later, Mary carried two plates with sandwiches over to the kitchen table. "Milk?" Bradley asked, standing next to the open fridge.

"Well, I would really like a diet…"

"Milk?" Bradley asked, interrupting her.

Sighing, she nodded. "Yes, fine, milk," she said.

He pulled the carton out of the fridge and then turned to her. "If you really want…"

She shook her head. "No, I really need to drink some milk today," she said with a sigh. She sat down at the table. "It's really good for me."

Bradley poured milk nearly to the top of the glass and put it on the counter while he turned to put the carton back in the fridge. "I'm really glad we haven't had any disturbing visits," he said, his head still behind the fridge door.

"Um, Bradley," Mary said, her voice shaking slightly.

The young woman in the beehive hair style stood on the other side of the counter, glaring at Mary. She looked at the full glass of milk, then looked at Mary, and the glare changed into an evil smile.

Mary shook her head. "No, not the milk," she said.

The glass jiggled on the counter. Bradley dove for it, but it was too late. The glass levitated into the air and floated toward Mary. Pushing her chair back, Mary tried to dodge the glass, but it was moving fast and locked on her like a heat-seeking missile. A moment later the contents of the glass splashed over Mary's head and dripped down over the rest of her body.

"That wasn't very nice," Mary said, shivering from having cold milk run down her back.

"He's mine," the ghost said. "And you can't have him."

"Listen," Mary said as milk dripped down from her hair into her face. "Can we just talk?"

"No," the ghost said, fading away. "Just remember. He's mine."

Bradley rushed over with several dish towels, handing several to Mary and wiping the milk off her back. "I'm so sorry, sweetheart," he said. "I'm so sorry."

She stopped blotting the milk from her hair for a moment and turned to look at him. "This is not your fault," she said. "This is nothing you did."

He sighed and shook his head. "I must have," he said. "Why else is she attached to me?"

"I don't know," she replied as she continued drying her hair. "But I'm rapidly losing my patience."

He took the damp towels from her and looked at his soaked wife. "Want some chocolate cake?" he asked.

She nodded. "Yeah, but I think I'll skip the milk this time."

Chapter Twenty-eight

The next morning, Mary's cell phone rang as she and Bradley were getting ready for work. "Hello," she said, answering the phone.

"Hi Mary, this is Renee from Computer Dynamics," Renee said. "Good news. We've rescued your information and uploaded it into a new laptop. You can pick it up anytime you'd like."

"Oh, that's great news," Mary replied. "I'll come by this morning on my way to work. Thank you, Renee. You guys are amazing."

"Just doing our job," Renee replied.

"Well, thank you," Mary said. "You just made my day."

She hung up the phone with a big smile on her face. "Good news?" Bradley asked, coming down the stairs.

"My new laptop is ready for me," she said. "And they were able to restore all of my information."

He bent over and kissed her. "That is good news," he said. "Are we going to submit an insurance claim for it?"

Mary grinned and shook her head. "I thought about it, for a second or two," she said, "until I tried to explain how the computer was damaged."

Bradley chuckled. "Yeah, I could see how that would be a problem," he said. "What else—"

He was cut off when Mary's phone rang again.

"Sorry," she said before answering her phone. "Hi, this is Mary."

"Mary, this is Sue from the Joiner Room in Sycamore," the voice on the other end of the phone said. "I found something this morning that I really think you ought to see."

"Okay," Mary said. "I've got a couple of meetings this morning, but I could probably be there by eleven. Will that work?"

"That will be perfect," Sue said. "I'll see you soon."

Mary hung up her phone and turned to Bradley. "Sue at the Joiner Room found something interesting," she said. "So I'm going to drive to Sycamore and look at it."

"Well, this worked out well," Bradley said.

"What do you mean?" Mary asked.

"I spoke to Ian yesterday, and he said he could meet me in Sycamore today at noon," Bradley explained. "I was going to tell you yesterday, but, well, the whole milk thing distracted me."

Mary chuckled. "Yeah, me too," she replied. "So is Rick on board?"

"Well, he thinks it's kind of weird," Bradley admitted. "But I told him it couldn't hurt and it just might help."

"Okay, so I'll get my computer, take care of a couple of things at the office and call you," Mary said.

An hour later, Mary was in her office, going through her emails on her new computer. She stopped when she heard the front door open. She watched Rosie and Margo walk in.

"Good morning," she said. "What a nice surprise."

"Oh, don't stand up," Rosie insisted when she saw Mary beginning to stand. "We'll sit down."

They hurried over to the seats in front of Mary's desk. "How are you feeling today?" Margo asked.

"I'm feeling good," Mary said. "Thank you for asking. How was your day yesterday?"

"Well, that's one of the reasons we came to see you," Rosie said. "Show her, Margo."

Margo pulled out the paper that Melvin had given them and laid it on the desk. "We received this yesterday," Margo explained. "From an acquaintance of Stanley's at the VFW. He put together a list of the people he thought could have killed Frasier and Shirley."

Mary looked down the paper. "Wow, this is quite a comprehensive list," she said. "I would never have even considered their paper carrier."

Margo smiled at Mary and nodded. "That's exactly what we thought," Margo said.

"It seemed to us that he's pretty eager to shift the blame," Rosie said. "Without thinking about the consequences."

"He could just be trying to impress both of you," Mary suggested.

"Yes, he could," Margo agreed, turning to look at Rosie. "Because he is that kind of person. And then there's another fellow at the VFW who seems to enjoy doing all he can to annoy the first fellow."

Mary smiled. "So you have two men who are trying to impress you?" she said.

Margo nodded. "And that's why we came up with our plan."

Mary didn't like the sound of that. "Your plan?" she asked.

Margo laughed. "Don't worry," she said. "We aren't going to do anything illegal."

"Well, that's a relief," Mary said with a smile.

"No, not this time," Rosie added with a wink at Mary.

"What's your plan?" Mary asked.

Margo leaned forward in her chair. "Well, it seems that the first fellow likes to impress the ladies," she said. "And he intimated that he would be happy to give me…" She wiggled her eyebrows. "More information about the list, if I wanted to meet with him."

"He was flirting with you?" Mary asked.

"Flirting would be a mild term," Rosie said. "He was practically throwing himself at her."

"So, we thought I could meet him," Margo said, "in a very public place and see if I could get him to let me know what he really thinks about their death."

"Very public?" Mary asked.

Rosie nodded. "Oh yes, very," she assured her. "And Stanley and I will be waiting outside for her."

Mary looked at Margo. "And you won't take any risks?"

Margo lifted her right hand and held it up. "Scout's honor," she said.

"And then she'll meet with the second fellow and see what she can find out about the first fellow," Rosie said.

Mary shook her head. "You're like a regular Mata Hari," Mary laughed.

"Yes, except I'd rather not be executed once I get the information," Margo replied drily.

"Oh, let's not have you be Mata Hari," Rosie exclaimed. "How about if you're Jessica Fletcher? She never dies."

Margo smiled at her friend. "That's a much better plan," she said.

"Well, whoever you are, I'd be very interested to see what you find out," Mary said.

"Dinner at your house tonight?" Rosie asked.

"That would be great," Mary said. "And we'll order in pizza so no one has to cook."

"Okay," Rosie said as both of the women stood up. "We'll see you tonight."

"See you then," Mary said. "And Margo…"

Margo stopped and looked at Mary. "Yes?"

"Be careful, okay?"

Margo smiled and nodded. "I will. I promise."

Chapter Twenty-nine

"So, Margo's daughter is a mystery writer?" Bradley asked as they drove towards Sycamore.

"Yeah, she writes paranormal mysteries," Mary replied. "And I really love them."

Bradley shook his head. "I've heard stories about writers, especially mystery writers," he said, shaking his head. "They can be kind of…" He paused as he searched for his words. "Odd. Yeah, that's the best way to describe it. Odd."

Mary shrugged and smiled at him. "You know, the same thing could be said about us," she said. "Oh, what did you do last night? Washed my hair because a poltergeist spilled milk on me. And what are you doing today? Going to a library to discover the identity of said poltergeist, hypnotizing someone who might have a spirit attached to them and then meeting with some friends to discuss another murder."

Bradley was silent for a moment and then sighed. "Okay, point taken," he said. "We're odd, too."

"All the best people are," she teased.

Once at the Joiner Room, Mary immediately brought Bradley to the counter and introduced him to

Sue. Once the introductions were over, Sue was anxious to show Mary what she'd discovered.

"Come over here to the back of the counter area," she invited.

They walked around the counter and found a yearbook, opened up, lying on the middle of the counter. "I found this here, this morning," Sue said. "And it wasn't here when I locked up last night. But look at this."

Mary bent over to look at the picture in the book. "It's her," Mary said, looking at a photograph of their poltergeist. "Julie Scott. She was a sophomore and a cheerleader."

She picked up the book. "What year is this?" she asked, turning the book over.

"It's 1965, the last year the old high school was in use," Sue said.

Mary shook her head. "But that doesn't make any sense," she said, putting the book back down on the counter. "Bradley wasn't born yet. Why would she attach herself to him?"

The pages of the book started to flutter. "I have a feeling we're going to find out why," Sue said, her voice just slightly shaky.

Mary could see that Mrs. Penfield had joined them at the counter and was quickly flipping through the pages. Finally, she stopped and smiled up at Mary. "That's why," she said, pointing to a photo.

Mary looked at the book and gasped. A photo of Bradley, dressed in a football uniform, was featured in the middle of the page. Mary looked at the caption. No, not Bradley Alden, Blake Alden, Bradley's father. "Your dad," she said, looking up at Bradley. "He looks just like you."

Bradley looked down at the photo. "Yeah, I can see the resemblance," he said. "So, you think Julie believes I'm my dad?"

"That's the only thing that makes sense," Mary replied, turning to Sue. "Did you happen…"

Sue smiled and handed Mary several pieces of paper. "You must deal with researchers a lot to understand that I would have already done a search for her."

Mary smiled back. "You just seem like a very thorough person," she replied.

Glancing down, Mary read the headlines from a May 1965 copy of the local paper. "Local Girl Dies in Rollover Accident."

She looked up at Bradley. "She was on her way to the prom when she lost control of her car," she said.

"Damn," he said shaking his head. "So, she's been waiting all this time."

Mary nodded. "Okay, now at least we know what happened," she said. "And now all we have to do is figure out how to fix it."

Chapter Thirty

Margo took a deep breath and then checked her reflection in the restaurant's glass door. *Good*, she thought, *I don't look as nervous as I feel.* Pushing against the door, she immediately smelled the familiar scents of a corner diner: hot coffee, deep fry grease and hamburger. The hostess was at the door greeting her immediately.

"Hi, booth for one?" she asked with a friendly smile.

"I'm meeting someone for lunch," Margo said, scanning behind the woman to see if Melvin was already there.

"Oh, are you meeting Mel?" the hostess asked.

Margo nodded. "Yes, I am."

She inclined her head towards the back. "He's back here," she said. "I'll show you."

They passed a few other tables with customers, passed the salad bar and finally arrived in the far corner of the room at a secluded booth. "Here we go," the hostess said.

Melvin stood up and smiled. "Margo, it's so wonderful to see you again."

"Hello, Melvin" she replied, hoping her smile reached her eyes. "Thank you for inviting me to lunch."

"Please, have a seat," he offered, waiting until she sat before he did. "Did you get a chance to look at the list I gave you?"

"Yes," she said, reaching into her purse and pulling it out. "It was quite comprehensive." She leaned forward and lowered her voice. "I really didn't know the Kochs very well," she said. "Passing acquaintances really. But this list paints an entirely different picture of them than I had. Did you know them very well?"

"Well, I'm fairly new to the area," he said. "I just moved here about ten years ago. But I think I have a pretty good instinct about people."

Margo nodded. "Do you?" she asked.

Sitting back in his seat with a self-satisfied look on his face, he nodded. "Yeah, some people might actually accidentally think that I was a detective," he said.

Margo bit back a smile. "Really? A detective?"

"Yeah, I've got a real knack about people, a real knack," he said.

"Well, perhaps we could go down this list," she said, sliding the list towards him. "Which of these people do you think would be on the top of your suspect list?"

Melvin looked down the list, a frown on his face. "Well, you know, I would hate to get any of these folks in trouble," he said.

"But if they killed Frasier and Shirley," Margo replied.

Melvin shrugged. "Well, really, I'm not too sure they killed anyone," he hedged.

"But I thought you gave me this list because you thought these people are potential suspects," she said.

Melvin cleared his throat and looked around the room. "Well," he said, turning back to Margo, "actually…"

He broke off when the waitress approached. "Oh, good," he said with a relieved sigh. "We should order." He turned his attention to the waitress. "What's the special today?"

"Meatloaf," the waitress replied. "One of our best sellers."

"That sounds great," Melvin said. "I'll take the meatloaf." He smiled at Margo. "How about you? My treat."

Margo turned to the waitress. "I'll have the chef salad," she said, "with ranch dressing on the side."

When the waitress left with their order, Margo turned to Melvin. "Melvin, do you actually have any idea of who could have killed Frasier and Shirley?" she asked.

He shrugged. "Well, you know, any of those people could have," he said. "I mean, anyone can be a murderer given the right motivation."

Margo paused as a chill ran down her spine. "What do you mean?"

Melvin looked away for a moment, as if he was gathering his thoughts. "You know, some people just want to be left alone," he explained. "Some people move somewhere new to, you know, start a new life. They don't need people looking at their past."

"Was Frasier looking into someone's past?" she asked.

His jaw tightened for a moment, and then he took a deep breath. He smiled tightly and shrugged. "Well, who knows what he was looking into," Melvin said easily. "And if he was, he took that information with him to the grave."

Chapter Thirty-one

Lunch seemed to take an eternity in Margo's point of view, but it was actually over within an hour. She thanked Melvin for his hospitality and insisted that she pay for her own meal. He actually looked relieved, and she was glad she'd taken Butch's advice and brought extra money.

She excused herself and went to the ladies room until Melvin left, and then she walked to the back of the restaurant to join Stanley and Rosie in their car.

"How did it go?" Stanley asked.

Margo shook her head. "That is one strange man," she said. "He's got some secrets that he desperately doesn't want anyone to find out about. But I don't know if he's capable of killing anyone."

"But what about the list?" Rosie asked. "What about all those names?"

"I think that list was a wild goose chase," Margo said. "When I tried to pin him down, he backed away from all of the names. I think it was more to impress me than to give us any solid evidence."

"So, it was a waste of time," Stanley said.

"Well," Margo said with a half-smile, "I had a very nice chef salad."

"And I bet you had to pay for it," Rosie said.

Margo nodded. "Yes, but I preferred it that way," she said. "I did not want to be beholden to him in any way. He does worry me a little. If he thought someone was looking into his background, he might do something drastic to protect himself."

Stanley started the car and pulled out of the parking lot. "Where to next?" he asked.

"The ice cream parlor on South Street," Margo said. "Not that I need ice cream."

Rosie laughed. "Don't worry. All this stress will burn off those calories," she said.

Margo chuckled. "Well if that isn't true, it should be."

A few minutes later, Stanley pulled into the parking lot and let Margo out. "We'll be right here," he said. "You get up and walk out if you feel uncomfortable. You don't owe nobody nothing."

"Thank you, Stanley," Margo said. "I'm sure this will be interesting."

She walked into the parlor and saw Butch sitting in a corner booth. Walking over to join him, she slipped in the booth across from him and sighed. "I just had the most interesting lunch with Melvin," she said immediately. "He was going to give me information about Frasier and Shirley Koch, but it turned out he didn't know them very well at all."

"That doesn't surprise me," Butch said. "I find that Melvin tends to be a bit of a windbag."

Margo smiled sympathetically. "Well, you know, I'm sure he meant well."

"But he wasted your time," Butch interrupted. "Wasted your time and probably tried to flirt with you."

Deciding that remaining silent would be the best response, Margo simply smiled.

"That's diplomatic of you," Butch laughed. "But we both know the guy's a loser."

"Did you know Frasier and Shirley?" Margo asked, changing the subject.

Butch's smiled widened, and he inhaled deeply, reminding Margo of a bantam rooster just before he's going to crow. "Well, to tell you the truth," he said,, "I knew Frasier better than his wife and…" He paused dramatically. "Not to speak ill of the dead, but Frasier was a bit of an egomaniac."

"Oh really?" Margo asked, widening her eyes to emphasize her interest while she slipped her hand into her pocket and started the small recording device Stanley had obtained for her. "An egomaniac?"

Butch nodded. "He always had to be in charge of everything," he said. "Head of the Chamber, head of the Rotary, and he wanted to run the VFW when he knew that position should have been mine."

"And I'm sure you were in the background doing all the work, and he was getting all the credit," Margo encouraged.

"Yes! Yes, exactly," Butch said. "I was always there, always helping, always making suggestions. But no one even noticed me when he was around." He shook his head sadly. "No one realized that my personality was just as good, my ideas were just as worthy, and my devotion to the cause was just as strong."

Margo slipped her hand across the table and covered Butch's hand with it. "Well, I've noticed," she said.

He smiled at her with such intensity, she nearly pulled her hand back and she was more than a little relieved when the waitress stepped up to get their order.

"Hi, what can I get you?" she asked.

"Well, we really haven't had a chance..." Butch began, turning his hand to try and capture Margo's hand in his own.

"I'll have a scoop of chocolate," Margo interrupted, grabbing the menu with both hands.

"A cone or a cup?" the waitress asked.

"A cup would be perfect," Margo replied.

"Got it," the waitress said. "And what about you?"

"I'll have a hot fudge sundae," Butch said, his voice holding a note of sulkiness. "And take your time."

Once the waitress left, Margo smiled across at him. "This is such a treat," she said, trying to soothe his ego. "I don't get to go out much in Deadwood."

Somewhat pacified, Butch smiled back. "Yeah, well, you should think about staying around here," he said. "I can guarantee that I would make sure you were always taken care of"

Margo quickly schooled her features so her dislike wouldn't show. "I can only imagine," she said. "You must be quite a man about town here in Freeport. Did you know Frasier all your life? Was he always such an attention hog?"

Butch nodded. "Yes," he said emphatically. "Yes. Exactly. All my life Frasier was around hogging all the attention. He was the quarterback; I was on the school paper. He was the lead in the play; I built sets. He was homecoming king; I stayed home."

166

"Oh, Butch, I'm so sorry," Margo said, understanding the man a little more. "It must have been hard to live in someone's shadows all those years."

His eyes snapped on hers with anger. "I was not in anyone's shadow," he insisted. "I held my own. I was important. I was smarter than he was. And that's what really counts, isn't it?"

Her heart jumped at the look in his eye and the intensity in his voice. She nodded meekly. "Yes, that's exactly what counts," she said, taking a deep breath and adding, "being cleverer than your opponent."

He smiled, and the expression made her skin crawl. "Yes," he said nodding. "That's it exactly. Being cleverer. Like trapping a small animal, you have to be patient, use the right bait and wait for the right time to move in for the kill."

She froze, her eyes wide with fear. She knew she should act normally, pass it off, but she just couldn't.

Butch stared at her for a moment, his eyes narrowing. "Margo, is anything wrong?" he asked slowly.

Taking a deep, unsteady breath, she shook her head. "No," she whispered, reaching for her water glass and taking a shaky sip.

"Are you sure?" he asked.

She placed the glass down, a little more in control, and nodded at him. "It's just that I'm such an animal lover, and the idea of something being trapped," she explained as she waved her hand in front of her eyes to dry the tears, "well, it nearly overcame me."

His smile softened. "Oh, don't worry," he assured her. "I would never do something like that to animals. They're harmless."

She nodded and swallowed audibly. "Yes, they are," she agreed. "Aren't they?"

Chapter Thirty-two

With the borrowed yearbook stored safely in the back of the car, Mary and Bradley drove over to Rick's house in one of the quiet, older, residential areas of Sycamore. They pulled up directly behind Ian's car, which was parked at the curb.

Before Bradley could turn off the car, Ian was at Mary's door, helping her out and enfolding her in a hug. "I kenna believe how beautiful you look," he said. "You are simply radiant."

"And you know just what a pregnant woman needs to hear," Mary replied, giving him another quick hug.

Ian stood back and placed his hand over his heart. "Darling, I'm only telling the God's own truth," he said. "You've always been a lovely woman, but now you just shine."

He glanced over at Bradley, who was walking around the car to join them. "And I'm hoping you've been telling her the self-same thing," he said.

Slipping his arm around Mary, Bradley nodded. "Every single day," he said. "Although I think she just believes it's false flattery coming from me."

Mary blushed. "Okay, enough, both of you," she said, uncomfortable with all the praise. "You're going to turn my head, and then I'll have an ego as big as my belly."

Ian chuckled and shook his head. "I won't believe that until I see it," he said. "Now, tell me a wee bit about your friend."

"I've known Rick since high school," Bradley said. "I guess he's always been sensitive. Although back in high school we just called it weird." He smiled at the memory. "Anyway, he was the one who told us his house was haunted, or that he could see things at the school. Or when we were camping, he told the ghost stories."

Ian nodded. "So, when did he seem to change?"

"When we were overseas," Bradley said. "In the Middle East."

"Aye, well, that's an ancient land that's seen its share of war and death," Ian said. "There are probably layers upon layers of residual spirits inhabiting the area." He paused and looked over to the house. "And, if you're sensitive to begin with, well then, the spirits are attracted to you."

"Do you think you can help him?" Mary asked.

"Well, darling, I'm going to try," Ian replied. "Shall we go up and see?"

Rick opened the door for them as they walked up the stairs. "Hi, I saw you meeting together on the sidewalk," he said, looking at Bradley for an explanation.

"We were talking about you," Bradley replied with a casual shrug. "Ian had a couple of questions about your..." He paused for a moment. "Paranormal I guess is the best word. Paranormal past. You know, how you used to see ghosts when you were younger."

Rick nodded and turned to Ian. "Hi, I'm Rick," he said.

"I'm Ian," he replied. "And I've been seeing ghosts since I was a wee lad, so we have a lot in common. I've spent years studying paranormal activity, trying to attach some scientific interpretation to what we're seeing and experiencing."

"Have you had any luck?" Rick asked.

Ian grinned. "No, we're still just the weird chaps," he said.

Rick laughed, and Mary could see the tension disappearing with the laughter.

"Well, that's good to know," Rick said. "So, what are you planning on doing to me?"

"Nothing that will involve wires, electrodes or torture devices," Ian teased.

"Well, that's a relief," Rick said.

"Aye, but what I'd like to do is hypnotize you," Ian said, his tone serious. "And bring you back to when you first felt the change in you. Perhaps we can find an event that you've buried in your subconscious that is making you feel unhappy."

Nodding slowly, Rick took a deep breath. "I'm a little worried," he said.

"Aye, it's a scary thing to be opening up wounds from the past," he replied. "And I'll not be upset if you decide you don't want to do this. But, I can tell you. If you want an answer, I believe this is the best way to start."

"Mary and I can step out," Bradley added, "if you feel like you'd want a more private session."

Rick shook his head. "No. No, actually, I would like it if you both stayed," he said. "Bradley, you understand where I came from, and many of my experiences I already shared with you. So you might be able to hear something that I never told you. Something that stands out. And Mary," he smiled at her, "I trust you. I want you here."

She walked over and took his hand. "Thank you," she said. "And I want you to be happy again."

He squeezed her hand, then let it go and turned to Ian. "Okay," he said. "What's next?"

Ian pointed to the couch in the living room. "Why don't you lay down on the couch and get yourself comfortable," he said. "And then we can get started."

Rick propped his head on a pillow and his feet on the arm of the couch and relaxed as if he were taking a Sunday afternoon nap. "This is good so far," he said.

Ian chuckled. "Now, I want you to close your eyes and relax," Ian said, his voice soothing and calm. "Let the worries you've been carrying slide away, off your shoulders, out of your mind and let them pool on the floor. No need to worry about them. You can pick them up later, if you'd like, but for now, just let them slide away."

Mary could see the muscles in Rick's shoulders loosen and his breathing change.

"Aye, that's grand," Ian said. "And now that those burdens are gone, I want you to float. Imagine yourself floating in a cloudless, blue sky, safe and secure, floating where no one and nothing can hurt you."

As Ian continued to speak, Mary watched Rick's breathing slow and become more rhythmic. He responded to Ian's questions in a soft, sleepy voice, on the edge between asleep and awake.

"Now, Rick, how are you feeling?" Ian finally asked.

"Relaxed," Rick replied. "Safe."

"Good, that's good," Ian said. "Now, let's go on a wee journey. You'll still be up in the sky, safe and protected, but you'll be able to look down on yourself and watch your life, just like a movie."

Rick nodded.

"Let's fly back to high school," Ian said. "What do you see?"

Rick smiled broadly. "The guys are down there with me," he said. "We're walking back from a football game. Alden is such a nerd."

Mary turned and smiled at Bradley.

"Well, that's not so surprising, is it?" Ian asked, winking at Mary. "And what is it your gang is doing?"

"We're going to cut through the cemetery on the way home," he said, the tone of his voice changing, becoming more serious. "The other guys want to cut through, but I don't want to."

"Why not?" Ian asked.

"I don't know," he said. "There's something…" He paused, and then he lifted his hand in his sleep and pointed. "There. I never saw it before, but there. That thing in the middle of the cemetery is waiting for us. Wants us to come."

His voice is excited and panicked. "We shouldn't go in there," he said, the fear evident. "We need to go back."

"What do you do?" Ian said.

"The other guys, the other guys are laughing at me," Rick said, shaking his head. "They start to climb the fence. But…" He pauses and then sighs, dropping his hand and relaxing. "Alden just told them he saw something in the trees and he's not going in. So, we're leaving. We're taking the long way."

"Did Alden see what you saw?" Ian asked, and Mary sent a questioning look at Bradley.

Bradley's quick shake of his head came at the same time Rick responded. "No, he didn't see anything," he said with gratitude in his voice. "He was just watching out for me."

Chapter Thirty-three

Ian had slowly guided Rick through his high school years, into college and boot camp, and now they were finally at the place in his memory where he thought the problem had started.

"Tell me what you see," Ian said.

"Desert and mountains," Rick said. "I see our FOB and the guys in my squadron."

"What's happening down there?" Ian asked.

"It's getting dark. It's my turn for sentry duty at the front gate," Rick said. "Me and Williams have duty together."

"Can you go down a little closer?" Ian asked. "Do you feel safe?"

Rick nodded. "Yeah, I can get closer," he replied. "We're walking to the guard hut."

"Is it a far walk?" Ian asked.

Rick nodded. "Yeah, about two city blocks," he said. "We're walking down a narrow lane. There's tall, chain-link fencing with barbed wire on top of it on either side of us. On the outside of the fencing is razor wire, so no one can get to the fence."

"Is it dark?" Ian asked.

"Yeah, the sun is setting," Rick replied. "There are tall, sentry lights, like street lights, every 100 yards. But the light only shines for about 30 yards in all directions, so you walk from light into dark and then back into light."

"Are you safe?" Ian asked.

Rick nodded again. "Yeah, we're safe," he said. "Williams is a good guy. I like having guard duty with him. We're doing the twelve to twelve overnight shift."

"Okay, so what's happening now?" Ian asked.

"It's later," Rick said. He paused, and Mary watched him sit up on the couch, his eyes still closed. "Something's out there."

He looked over his shoulder. "Hey, Williams, someone is out there," he said. "I'm going out."

Standing, Rick walked across the room, his eyes still closed, and watched something unseen for a few moments. "It's just a villager," he called over his shoulder. "He must have been working late at the FOB. Some really old guy."

Walking back to the couch, Rick sat down, but still watched. "He's going dark," he said. "He'll be in light in a few moments."

He continued to watch and wait.

"He's not coming out," he called. "What the hell? He's not coming out. Williams did you see him?"

Agitated, Rick scans the room. "There's no place he could have gone," he said, his voice frantic. "Where the hell is he?"

"Rick, are you still safe?" Ian asked, interrupting him.

Shaking his head, Rick continues to scan the area. "No, I'm not safe," he said. "The old guy, he's gone."

"Okay, go back up to the sky, Rick," Ian commands him. "Go up right now and look down."

Laying back down on the couch, Rick's breathing calms, but he's still looking around. "I see myself," he said. "I see myself with Williams. Dammit!"

"What?" Ian asked, his voice still soft, but Mary could hear the tension in it. "What do you see?"

"The old guy," Rick said, his voice confused. "The old guy is next to me, but I don't see him. He's right there, next to me, and he's smiling."

He shivered, and Mary felt a chill run down her spine.

"He's next to me," Rick said. "And now..." He paused and shook his head. His breathing became shallow, and his voice was a frightened whisper. "The old guy," he said, his voice shaking, "I think he's inside of me."

Chapter Thirty-four

Rick sat on the couch, his elbows on his knees and his head cradled in his hands. "I can remember it," he said slowly. He looked up at Ian. "Am I supposed to remember it?"

Ian shrugged. "Well, it really wasn't too far down in your subconscious," he said. "So, since we just kind of shined a psychological light on those memories, there's no reason you shouldn't remember it."

"Well, okay, so now what do I do with it?" he asked. "I feel like I'm part of a science fiction movie and something is going to come exploding out of my body any moment."

"I totally understand that feeling," Mary said with a smile, looking down at her belly.

Rick was taken aback for a moment and then chuckled. "Okay, I guess you do," he said. "But, I've got to admit, I'm more than a little freaked out."

"I can imagine," Ian said. "So, the first thing I need to ask you is, do you want this old guy unattached from you?"

Rick looked confused. "Of course I do," he said. "Why would you even ask that question?"

"Because he's been with you for over a decade," Ian said. "And if you don't really want him to go, I don't want to even try."

"No, I want him to go," Rick said emphatically. "I want my life back. I really want to be happy."

"Okay," Ian said. "Do you remember any Farsi?"

Rick nodded. "Yeah, I still remember a little."

"Okay," Ian said. "You need to concentrate on a mental image of the old man and ask him to come out of you, so you can meet him."

"Wait. What?" Rick said. "You want me to meet some demon thing that's been taking over my body? What if he's dangerous?"

"Most of the time, when you have spirit attachments like this," Ian said, "it's not a possession. Generally, you have spirits who are lost and confused. Because you are open and sensitive, because you could see him, he gravitated to you. But, he brought with him the sadness and confusion of his death. We just need to help him go on his way."

"Really?" Rick asked, releasing a sigh of relief. "That's it?"

Ian nodded. "Generally, yes, that's it," he said. "So, let's see if we can talk to him and help him."

Rick made the request in Farsi for the old man to come out and meet them. They waited for a few moments, but nothing happened. Rick repeated the request, and Mary thought she saw a shadow form around Rick. But it slipped back in again.

"I thought I saw something," Mary said.

"He's been with you a long time," Ian said. "It might be hard for him to make the separation."

"Can I try?" Mary asked.

"That might be a good idea," Ian said. "Mary's the least intimidating of all of us in the room."

Rick nodded. "Give it a shot."

She repeated the words Rick had said, slowly and gently. Then, in English she added, "Please don't be afraid. We just want to help you go home."

The outline of a shadow appeared next to Rick, wavering and undulating, like a heat wave. It got more pronounced, and finally, a diminutive, dark-skinned man appeared next to Rick on the couch. He cowered into the cushions as he gazed around the room.

"We're here to help you," Mary said. "Can you understand me?"

The elderly man appeared confused. Rick turned and spoke to the man in Farsi, his voice gentle and kind. The man smiled and nodded at Rick.

"He needs to remember what happened before he died," Ian said. "He needs to understand that he is no longer alive."

Rick turned back to him and spoke. The old man's eyes widened, and then his gaze became thoughtful. Finally, he spoke quickly, his hands gesturing wildly.

"He worked in the FOB for us, the American soldiers," Rick said. "As did many in his village. They liked the Americans. They wanted peace. But the Taliban found out they were working for us and decided to punish the village."

Rick looked up and nodded. "I remember that happening," he said. "It was just before we got there. The Taliban killed about 100 villagers in the next village over."

He turned back to the man and spoke to him. The old man sat quietly, listening, taking Rick's words in, and then he looked up, tears in his eyes and looked at Mary. "I am dead?" he asked in broken English.

Mary nodded, tears filling her eyes. "Yes," she whispered. "I'm so sorry. But, yes, you are dead."

He put his hands out in front of his face and shook his head. "I did not know these things."

"What is your name?" Mary asked.

"Hadi," the man replied.

"Hadi," Mary repeated. "It is time for you to move on. Are you ready?"

He nodded slowly. "Yes," he said. "Yes. I do."

She wiped a stray tear from her cheek and nodded. "Good. Now you must look around you," she said. "And look for a bright light."

Hadi slowly searched the room, then stopped, his eyes widening once again. He whispered something in Farsi.

"He said it is beautiful," Rick translated.

Mary nodded. "It is beautiful," she said. "And now, Hadi, you need to walk towards it. Your friends and family are waiting for you there. They've waited a long time."

He stood and took three steps and then faded out of sight.

Rick glanced quickly around the room. "He's gone?" he asked incredulously.

Ian nodded. "Yes, he's gone," he said. "How do you feel?"

Rick paused and thought about it for a moment. A wide smile appeared on his face. "I feel great," he said, shaking his head in disbelief. "I feel… I can't even describe it. I feel new."

Bradley walked over and gave his friend a hug. "Nice to have you back," he said.

"Amazing to be back," Rick replied. Then he turned to Ian and gave him a hug. "Thank you. Thank you so much."

"You're welcome," Ian said. "And, if you wouldn't mind, I'd love to stay in touch with you and make sure there are no residual effects."

"No, I don't mind at all," he said. "That would be great."

Rick walked across the room to Mary. "Thank you," he said, emotion choking his voice. "Thank you for helping me become happy again."

She hugged him. "You are so welcome," she replied. "I am so happy for you."

He took a deep, unsteady breath and let it out slowly. "Okay, so what's next?" he asked with a grin.

"Ian's never tried a Chicago-style hot dog," Mary said.

Rick turned to Ian, a look of amused shock on his face. "What?" he asked. "Well, we have to fix that immediately." He grabbed his jacket from the coat rack and walked to the door. "Come on, everyone, lunch is on me."

Chapter Thirty-five

Mary sighed happily as Bradley drove through Freeport, back towards their house. "This was a great day," she said.

Bradley nodded as he maneuvered down the side streets. "I agree," he said. "I can't remember when I've seen Rick happier. It was like the final scene of A Christmas Carol when Scrooge is giddy with happiness. I always thought that scene was kind of weird, but now I understand it."

Mary nodded thoughtfully. "I can't imagine being caught under a blanket of that much unhappiness," she said. "And I know that there are people suffering through depression who see the world that way every day."

"Yeah, but how tough would it be suffering through someone else's depression?" Bradley asked, glancing over at her. He turned the car down their street and shook his head. "No rest for the wicked."

Mary looked ahead. "What?" she asked.

"Rosie and Stanley's car is parked in front," he said. "I'm sure they're waiting for us."

"Oh, that's right. I forgot," she said. "Pizza at our house tonight."

Bradley looked over at her. "Chicago hot dogs and fries for lunch and pizza for dinner?" he asked. "Are you sure?"

She grinned at him. "I'll make mine thin crust with spinach and artichokes," she replied. "With a salad." She paused for a moment. "But only if you get the same."

Chuckling, he reached over and kissed her. "I will be happy to get the same," he said.

Bradley came around and helped Mary out of the car, and before they were across the driveway, Stanley, Rosie and Margo were at their side.

"I'm so glad you finally got home," Rosie said. "We have some very interesting information."

"I think they're wrong, iffen you want to know the truth," Stanley grumbled.

"I'm not wrong," Margo replied. "And you weren't there. It was frightening."

"Why don't we all just go inside and talk about it?" Bradley suggested. "And then we can order the pizza."

They hurried inside, and while Bradley went into the kitchen to order, Margo and Rosie surrounded Mary on the couch.

188

"Melvin did it," Margo said. "I know he did."

"And when she told me what he said, I agree with her," Rosie added.

Stanley sat across from them in the chair, his hands folded over his chest. "And I'm saying you got no proof other than he was jealous of Frasier," he said. "Lots of people are jealous, and they don't go killing folks."

Margo looked over at Stanley and shook her head. "But not lots of people have that same expression on their face," she said. "And the same tone to their voice. It was as if the person I was having lunch with changed. I tell you it gave me goosebumps."

"Why was he jealous?" Mary asked.

"He said that Frasier showed him up in every aspect of his life," Margo said. Then. Then she paused. "Well, he didn't put it in those words. I did. But basically since they were boys, Frasier was the one who came out on top."

"But that happens to lots of folks," Stanley said. "Especially in small towns. You get the leaders and you get the…"

He stopped himself before he said the final word.

"Losers?" Rosie asked.

189

"Well, I didn't want to say that," Stanley said.

"But that's what you thought, wasn't it?" Margo asked. "And how would you feel if all of your life you were known as the loser?"

Stanley grumbled for a moment and shook his head. "Well, I wouldn't like it," he said. "But I wouldn't go out and kill people. I'd work hard to make myself better."

Rosie leaned forward and placed her hand on Stanley's knee. "That's because you're a leader, dear," she said. "And you don't let anything get in your way. Not everyone is like that."

"I still don't think he'd do it," Stanley murmured.

"Well, how about Melvin?" Rosie asked. "He could have done it, too."

Mary shook her head. "Melvin? Who's Melvin?"

"He's the man who took over for Frasier at the VFW," Stanley said.

"He told me that anyone could commit murder," Margo said. "Especially if they felt threatened."

"And did he feel threatened?" Mary asked.

Margo nodded. "He said something about people doing a background check on him and not minding their own business."

Mary sighed. "Well, then we have three good suspects," she said.

"Three?" Stanley asked. "Who's the third?"

"It looks like Eddie is still in the running," Mary replied.

"Well, we need to start eliminating the possibilities," Margo said.

Stanley looked shocked. "We ain't eliminating no one," he said. "I don't go for murdering folks."

Margo rolled her eyes. "No, not that," she replied. "But we need to see if there is anything that would link them to the murder."

Mary glanced over to the kitchen where Bradley was still on hold with the pizza parlor, and then she turned back to Margo, Rosie and Stanley. "Well, there's one way we could be sure," she said, lowering her voice.

"How?" Margo asked.

"We could look for evidence in their homes," Mary replied.

"Shouldn't you be getting a warrant to do that?" Stanley asked.

Mary shrugged. "No one thinks a crime's been committed," she replied. "The authorities think it was bad driving. And the case has been closed for months. There's no way we could get a judge to issue us a warrant."

Stanley thought about it for a moment and then sighed. "Okay, Shirley and Frasier were friends of mine," he said. "What do you want to do?"?"

"Well, do you think we could try and get to all of them tomorrow? Mary asked.

Stanley nodded. "Melvin spends his Thursday mornings at the Senior Center, so his place will be empty all morning."

"Excellent," Mary said. "We can go there first. Stanley, I want you to be the lookout."

He nodded. "Okay, and after Melvin's?" he asked.

Mary looked over her shoulder once again. "I need you to take Butch to lunch tomorrow," she said to Stanley, "while the rest of us look for evidence."

"You're going to—" Stanley shouted until Rosie slapped his leg. He looked around, abashed and lowered his voice. "You're going to break into his house?"

"No one locks their doors around here," Mary said. "We're just going to walk in, not break in."

Stanley leaned forward. "What if he locks his doors?" he asked softly.

Mary met his eyes. "Plausible deniability, Stanley," she said. "You don't want to know."

She paused and looked up over their heads at Bradley, who was speaking on the phone. "But if you want to stop by his house this evening for a moment," Mary whispered, "and, "and if Rosie wants to accidentally forget her gloves, that wouldn't be a bad idea."

Stanley shook his head. "And what about Eddie?" he asked.

"Since Bradley already knows about him, we can leave him alone," she said. "Besides, I think your two are risky enough."

"That's what I'm afraid of," Stanley said with a sigh. Then he nodded. "Iffen he catches us," he shrugged his head in Bradley's direction, "you remember. This wasn't my idea."

Chapter Thirty-six

Once the pizza was eaten, Stanley, Rosie and Margo didn't stay very long. Mary suspected it was because they were afraid they would let something slip in front of Bradley. As it was, Mary was having a hard time not telling him what they were planning. But, if they got caught and he knew about it, Mary reasoned, it would cause trouble at the police station. And the fact that if he knew he would tell her not to do it—well, she didn't even want to go there.

"So, did you solve their issues?" Bradley asked as they tidied the kitchen.

Mary smiled and nodded. "Yes, I think so," she replied. "Aren't they just cute together?" She asked, trying to change the subject.

He paused, the dishtowel in one hand, and studied her. "You wouldn't be trying to avoid my questions, would you?"

Several replies ran through Mary's mind. *"Why yes, dear, I am." "No. Of course not." "How about those Bears?" "Look! It's a distraction!"*

But, she was saved from uttering a word by the ringing of Bradley's cell phone. He pulled it out of his pocket and answered. "Hi," he said with a smile. "We were just finishing up in the kitchen and were going to call you."

He mouthed "the Brennans" to Mary.

"Yes, we'll be right over," he said. He hung up the phone and put it away. "Ready to head over?"

Mary nodded. "Yes, I am so excited to see Clarissa," she said. "But then, when we get home, let's take some time with the yearbook. I would really like to get the extra company out of our house so we can get our little girl back home."

Bradley nodded. "Yes, good idea," he said. "It's a little too quiet in this house without the pitter patter of little feet."

She laughed. "Or the laughing and shouting of not-so-tiny lungs," she added.

"Agreed," he laughed. "Ready to go?"

"Ready!"

They spent the evening with the Brennans, playing board games and listening to Clarissa's adventures at school. By eight o'clock Clarissa and Maggie were both yawning widely and having a hard time keeping their eyes open.

"I think it's time for you to go to bed," Mary said, pulling Clarissa into her arms and hugging her. "I love you so much."

Clarissa snuggled against her. "I love you, too," she said. "I'm having fun here at the Brennans, but when can I come home?"

Mary sighed. "We're working on it, sweetheart," she said. "And I think we got a really good lead today. Your dad and I are going to work on it some more tonight."

"Okay," Clarissa replied, yawning again. "And then Maggie can stay at our house."

Mary chuckled. "Yes, she can," she said.

While Clarissa said goodnight to her father, Katie walked over to Mary. "How are you feeling?" she asked.

"Actually, I'm feeling good," she said. "I just wish we could get rid of the poltergeist. Last night I got a milk bath, courtesy of our unwanted visitor."

"Oh, Mary, that sounds both frightening and messy."

Mary laughed. "And cold," Mary added. "It was right out of the refrigerator cold."

"What an evil ghost," Katie said. "The least she could have done was warm it up a little."

Mary chuckled. "Actually, she's not evil," she said. "Just hurt and confused. I think we may have the lead we need to move her on."

"Well, I certainly hope so," Katie said. "You and Bradley need your home back."

"Yes we do," Mary agreed. "And we need it back soon."

Chapter Thirty-seven

The house was quiet when they arrived home a little later that night. Mary went into the kitchen to put the kettle on to make tea while Bradley started a fire in the fireplace. Once she filled the kettle with water and placed it on the burner, she turned to go to the cupboard and found herself face to face with the poltergeist.

Mary gasped as she looked into eyes that were blazing with anger, and the ghost smiled at her fear. "You should be afraid," she hissed. "You don't belong here with him."

Taking a calming breath, Mary stopped herself from backing away. "I'm not your enemy, Julie," Mary said firmly. "I want to help you."

The ghost's eyes widened at the mention of her name. "What did you call me?" she hissed.

"Julie. Julie Scott," Mary said. "You're a sophomore at Sycamore High School."

This time, the ghost stepped back and stared at Mary in surprise. "No one has called me that in a long time," she whispered.

"I want to—" Mary began.

"No!" Julie screamed. "No! Don't try to trick me."

Bradley ran into the kitchen. "Mary," he called, his heart dropping when he saw the ghost threatening her. But she quickly glanced toward him and shook her head. She didn't want him to interfere, not yet. Taking a step back, he waited, ready to jump in at a second's notice.

Mary turned back to Julie. "I'm not—" Mary tried again.

"Shut up! Just shut up!" Julie cried. She turned to look at Bradley. "You were supposed to love me."

"Julie," Bradley began.

"That's all I wanted," she cried, translucent tears slipping down her cheeks. "All I wanted."

She faded away before either of them could say anything else. Mary turned to Bradley and shook her head. "She's so sad," she whispered.

"Do you think she's gone for good?" Bradley asked, hurrying to her side and pulling her into his arms.

"I don't think so," Mary said, looking up at him. "I hope not."

Bradley looked surprised. "What? You hope not?"

"Her problem isn't resolved," she explained. "She still hasn't crossed over."

He nodded and hugged her. "I just want you to be safe," he said. "Helping Julie is important, but not as important as your safety."

She laid her head on his chest and sighed. She knew helping Julie cross over was her job, not Bradley's, and protecting her and their family was his. She wouldn't argue, wouldn't explain how important it was for her to do what she did. All she would do is accept his protection, his concern and his love. "I love you," she said softly.

He laid his cheek on the top of her head and held her tighter. "I adore you," he replied. "You are my world."

They stayed together until the screaming of the kettle made them pull apart.

She smiled up at him. "Tea or hot chocolate?" she asked.

He pressed his lips to her forehead. "Tea would be perfect," he said. "Something calming."

She smiled and nodded. "Okay, you check on the fireplace, and I'll be in there in a few minutes," she said.

She busied herself making the tea and then carried the mugs out to the coffee table in front of the couch. The fire was crackling, and the room was already warm and cozy. "Okay, this is perfect," she said, curling up in the corner of the couch with her mug in her hands.

Bradley sat next to her and nodded. "Yeah, this is nice," he said. He opened the yearbook up and started flipping through the pages. To Mary's amazement, Bradley's father's photo was featured on almost every other page in the book.

"Good grief," she said. "Your dad was like superman."

Bradley nodded, but he didn't smile. "Yeah, you're right. He was."

She put her hand over his to stop him from turning to the next page. "Tell me," she said.

He shook his head and shrugged. "It's nothing," he said. But she kept her hand over his.

"It's something," she said. "Tell me."

"I don't know," he said. "I'm looking at these pictures of a man I didn't know. I didn't get to know."

"I don't understand," Mary said.

Bradley leaned back and looked up to the ceiling for a moment. Then he turned and looked at her. "When I watch you with your family, the love you share, the support you give each other," he said softly, shaking his head, "I don't know if you realize how lucky you are."

He stopped for a moment to gather his thoughts. "I didn't really get to know my dad very well," he said. "I think part of it was because I wasn't the son he wanted."

"That's ridiculous," Mary said, defending Bradley from his father. "You're amazing."

He reached over and kissed her head. "Thank you," he said. "You are my staunchest defender. But, it wasn't bad. It wasn't abusive. I just felt like I never quite lived up to the Alden legacy. I was an ordinary student, not the valedictorian. I was a team player, not the star. I was on the swim team, not the football team. And then he and Mom died in a car accident when I was a senior, so I kind of always felt I never got the chance to prove him wrong."

Mary shook her head. "No, he would have been proud of the man you became," she said. "I'm sure of it."

Bradley sighed. "Well, that's nice of you," he said. "But I'm not as sure as you. And, you know, that's okay. I'm okay. I've got you and Clarissa and soon little Mikey. I've got so much to be grateful for, and I know it. Just, right now, you know…"

"It's tough?" Mary asked.

He nodded. "Yeah, it's a little tough," he said.

Mary moved her hand and closed the yearbook. "Come on," she said, putting her mug down, taking his hand and standing up.

"What?" he asked.

She smiled down at him. "I want you to take me upstairs," she said. "And dance with me."

"Dance with you?" he asked, surprised. "But I thought, you know, Julie…"

"I don't think she's coming back tonight," Mary said. "Besides, she's interested in your dad. I want the pick-of-the-litter, as Mrs. Penfield said."

Bradley stood up, and Mary led him to the stairs. She climbed up two stairs so they were at eye level with each other, turned, wrapped her arms around his neck and kissed him for all she was worth. When the kiss ended, she was slightly breathless. "Will you dance with me?" she whispered breathlessly.

He cradled her cheeks in his hands, stepped onto the first step and lowered his face to hers. "Try and stop me," he replied, crushing her lips beneath his own.

Chapter Thirty-eight

"Hello, Rosie," Mary said into the hands-free phone device in her car when Rosie answered it. "This is Mary."

"Mary, it's only seven o'clock," she said. "What's wrong?"

"Sorry, Rosie," Mary replied. "Nothing's wrong. I had to drive to Sycamore this morning, and I wanted to let you know. I think I can make it back by noon, but if Stanley could arrange a later lunch with Butch, that would be great."

"I'm sure he can," Rosie assured her. "Last night, when we stopped by, Stanley left the timing kind of loose because he wanted to check with you."

"Tell Stanley I think he's brilliant," Mary said.

Rosie laughed. "I don't know if I will," she teased. "He might get too big of a head with those kinds of compliments." Rosie paused for a moment. "Is everything okay?"

"Yes. Fine," Mary said. "I just needed to meet with someone this morning, that's all."

"Okay, well, just let us know when you're on your way back," she said. "And then we'll set things up."

"Thank you," Mary said. "I'll call you in a couple of hours."

She disconnected with Rosie and slowed down as she got closer to her destination. After her conversation with Bradley, she was hoping to get a little more help in solving this problem. She woke early in the morning knowing what she needed to do.

"I can't believe you're up, dressed and driving this early in the morning," Mike said as he appeared in the passenger seat next to her.

"Believe it," she said, proud of herself for not jumping when he appeared.

He leaned back in the seat. "So, where are we going?" he asked.

"To a cemetery," she replied. "I thought it would be an interesting change if I went to the spirits instead of the spirits always having to come to me."

"Ha ha," Mike replied and watched as they turned into the Sycamore Cemetery. "So, how many people do you think are dead in there?"

Mary rolled her eyes and turned to him. "All of them," she said. "That is such a dad joke."

Mike chuckled. "Yeah, I know."

She drove onto the paved road that led to the different sections of the cemetery.

"Turn left up here," Mike instructed.

Mary shot him a quick look. "How do you know…"

He smiled at her. "Because that's where I'd be going if I were you," he said gently. "Pull over there and park."

She did as he suggested, turned off the car, and in the early morning fog walked down a narrow path to a bench placed in front of a group of graves. She sat down and looked at the gravestone in front of her. "Jeannine Alden"

"Hi," she said. "I don't know if you can hear me, but I thought I'd give it a try. You knew Bradley back in high school. You knew his dad. And I was hoping you could help me with a problem we've got."

She related the story about Julie and what had happened in their home. "I want to help her," she finally said. "But I'm not sure I know how."

Suddenly Mary felt warmth coming from beside her. She turned to find Jeannine's spirit sitting next to her.

"Hi," Mary said. "Sorry I haven't come before."

Jeannine shook her head. "You know as well as I do that I'm not in that grave," she said. "But I do visit when family come to pay their respects. It's nice to catch up."

She studied Mary for a moment. "A baby?" she asked, her eyes filled with delight.

Mary put her hands on her abdomen and nodded. "A boy," she replied. "We're naming him Michael."

"That's wonderful," she said.

"Clarissa is happy," Mary said. "She is such a joy."

Jeannine nodded. "I know," she said. "I love watching over her. You're doing a wonderful job."

"I'm trying, sometimes failing," she admitted. "But I love her."

"I know you do," Jeannine said. "And she loves you. That makes me feel wonderful."

Mary looked at the gravestone for a moment and then turned back to the spirit. "It doesn't make you upset?" she asked.

"No. I'm only happy that my little girl has a mother who loves her," Jeannine said. "I'm grateful to you."

Mary shook her head. "I'm grateful to you for sharing her with me," she said.

Jeannine laughed. "Well, it's nice that we have a mutual admiration society," she said. "But my time with you is short, so let's talk about your problem. When Bradley moved in, did he bring a big, wooden, locker box?"

Mary nodded. "Yes, it's down in the basement."

"Excellent," she said. "It's got some of his dad's things from high school. I think it even has his dad's old letterman sweater. Now this is what I think you ought to do…"

She leaned over and whispered into Mary's ear. Mary listened intently, nodding occasionally, and finally laughed. "I think it will work," Mary said. "Thank you."

"Give Clarissa a hug from me," Jeannine said as she started to fade away. "And be patient with yourself. You're doing a great job."

"Thank you," Mary whispered as Jeannine disappeared.

She sat on the bench for another moment, letting Jeannine's advice sink in.

"Did she help you?" Mike asked.

Mary nodded and then looked at him. "Did you pull some strings?" she asked.

He shrugged. "She wanted to help," he said. "It wasn't hard."

"Thank you," Mary said.

She stood up, but instead of walking back to the car, she walked over to the other gravestones in the same area. She stopped in front of the one bearing the name "Blake Alden" and studied it for a moment.

"I don't mean to be disrespectful," she said to the grave. "Especially since we've never met. But if what Bradley believes is correct, that somehow you felt that he didn't live up to the Alden legacy, then you were sadly mistaken. Your son is one of the best men I've ever met in my life. He is honorable, brave and loyal. He loves with all his heart, and he protects the people he loves." She stopped and sighed softly. "I just wanted to let you know."

Turning, her shoes crunching on the gravel path, she walked back to her car in silence. She got into the car and sat there for a few moments, her hands on the steering wheels, staring out at the fog rolling over the grounds.

"Why?" she finally asked, whisking a tear from her cheek.

Mike appeared in the seat next to her. "Because when we're alive we don't always remember the important things like love and family," he said. "We get caught up in temporary things we think are important. Who's right. Who's better. Who's more important. Who makes more money."

He turned away from her and looked out the window at the acres of headstones. "It's not until we're dead that we realize we spent a whole lot of our time on things that really didn't matter in the long run."

"That's so sad," Mary said, turning on her car and pulling out onto the driveway.

Mike nodded. "Yes it is," he agreed with a sigh. "Yes it is."

Chapter Thirty-nine

"Are you sure Melvin's not going to be home?" Mary asked they pulled up in Stanley's car in front of the apartment complex.

"Melvin always goes to the Senior Center on Thursday morning," Stanley said. "He and his friends play cards until the noon meal."

Mary looked over at the car's clock. It was only nine-thirty. They had plenty of time. "Okay," she said. "Let's see what we can do."

They walked from the car up to the apartment building, and Mary casually looked around. "It's pretty deserted here," she said. "Do you think his apartment is unlocked?"

"Not likely," Stanley said.

"Oh, don't worry," Margo said, pulling a wrapped package from her purse. "I came prepared." She looked around. "Meet me at the back door. I'll let you in."

"Are you sure?" Mary asked.

Margo nodded. "Jessica Fletcher, remember?" she teased.

Leaving Margo, they walked around to the back of the building.

As soon as they were out of sight, Margo knocked on the door next to Melvin's apartment. An elderly man answered the door. "Can I help you?" he asked.

Margo smiled at him. "I certainly hope so," she said. "I was supposed to meet Melvin here this morning. I've been knocking for several minutes, but he doesn't answer."

"Well, this is his Senior Center day," the man said.

"Oh," Margo made a sound of distress. "I'm leaving in an hour, and I wanted to give him this little gift. He bought me lunch yesterday."

"Oh, are you the gal he was telling me about?"

She smiled. "I'm from Deadwood," she said.

"Yes. Yes, he was telling me about you," he said.

She looked around, feigning desperation. "Is there a manager I could speak with?" she asked. "I just want to leave this gift for him and…" She looked embarrassed. "Leave him a little note since I can't tell him how I feel in person."

"Well, I've got his key," he said. "I can let you in."

"Oh, are you sure?" she asked. "I really don't want to break any rules."

"What?" the man asked. "Melvin told me all about you. He'd be as disappointed as hell if I didn't let you in."

He went back into his apartment, grabbed a key hanging on a hook near the door and came outside. "Here you go," he said, unlocking the door and pushing it open. "Just lock the door behind you when you leave."

"Thank you," she said, allowing her eyes to mist. "You don't know what this means to me."

He smiled at her. "Well, all I can say is that Melvin's a lucky guy."

She stepped inside. "I'll lock up," she said. "I promise. Thanks again."

She closed the door behind her and walked through the cluttered apartment to the back door. "Hurry," she whispered as she waved them in.

"How did you…" Mary started to ask.

"I'll tell you later," Margo said. "But we only have a little while."

Once they were all inside, they looked around and were surprised that, despite the clutter, there was very little in the apartment.

"It looks like he's got a twin bed and a small dresser," Stanley said, standing outside the bedroom door. "But that's about it."

"He has no kitchen table," Rosie said. "Only a TV tray and a folding chair."

"And this is just a one-bedroom apartment," Margo said. "So, he isn't hiding a computer. He just doesn't have one."

"Does he have a car?" Mary asked.

Stanley thought about it for a moment. "No. I think he takes the Senior Bus everywhere he goes," he said.

Looking around the apartment, Mary shook her head. "I don't see how he could even get to the Koch's house to tamper with their car," she said. "And I don't see any tools anywhere."

"He's destitute," Rosie said. "That's why he was embarrassed about people looking into his background."

"I really think we can take him off the list," Mary said.

Margo nodded. "And I think I'll go back next door and leave this gift with his neighbor," she said.

"He doesn't need to know that someone was in his apartment."

Chapter Forty

An hour later, Mary parked her car around the corner from Butch's house and then turned to Rosie. "Are we really sure—" she began.

"It's the only way," Margo inserted. "I don't even know the couple you are trying to help, but I believe that justice needs to be served."

Sighing, Mary turned off the car and nodded. "You're right," she said. "I just wish we didn't have to break the law to do it."

"Oh," Rosie said with a sudden smile. "We're not breaking the law. I forgot to tell you."

"What?" Mary asked.

"Last night, when I left my glove there," Rosie said, "Butch told me that I could drop by anytime. I was always welcome. So, we're just dropping by, not breaking in."

Mary smiled and shook her head. "I'm sure he meant when he was home," she said.

Rosie shrugged. "Well, he didn't say that," she reasoned. "So, we are just dropping by. It's perfectly legal."

"Besides," Margo added. "we're old. We get confused."

Mary turned to look at Margo in the back seat. "I'm not old," she said.

Margo smiled. "You're pregnant," she said. "Same difference. The hormones do crazy things to your brain."

Mary laughed. "Well, now that we've covered all the legal areas, we might as well go in."

Rosie and Margo nodded in agreement. "Let's go," Margo said.

The neighborhood was quiet, all the neighbors either at work or busy inside their homes. The three women had no problem walking up onto the front porch, opening the unlocked door and letting themselves in. "See," Rosie whispered. "We didn't have to break or enter."

"Well, we didn't have to break," Mary whispered back as they stood in Butch's hallway. "But we certainly have entered."

Rosie looked around. "Oh, yes, you're right."

"So, where do we start?" Margo asked, pulling a pair of latex gloves out of her pocket and slipping them on.

"You brought gloves?" Mary asked.

Margo dug through her purse and pulled out two more pair. "I brought extra," she said. "Just in case they dust the place for fingerprints."

Mary looked at both of the women. "We're not going to kill anyone or steal anything," she said. "So I don't think they're going to need to dust."

"You never know," Margo replied, handing a pair to Mary.

With a resigned shrug, Mary slipped the gloves on her hands and then looked around the house. "Why don't we see if he has an office?" Mary suggested. "That might be the best place to start."

They walked through the living room that had plates, cups and silverware scattered around it. Rosie walked over to the coffee table that had a plate with the remains of breakfast on it. She shook her head and picked up the plate. "It really doesn't take any time at all to just pick things up and wash them off," she said.

"What are you doing?" Margo asked.

"I'm cleaning up..." Rosie began.

"Rosie, we're breaking and entering," Margo reminded her. "We're not supposed to be cleaning up."

Rosie looked down at the plate and then back at Margo. "But it's disgusting," she said.

"Put the plate back," Margo insisted.

Slowly lowering the plate to the table, Rosie sighed. "Fine."

They walked down the hall, and Mary peeked into the kitchen. It was a mess. "Don't even look in that direction, Rosie," Mary said, turning her friend away from the doorway. "It will ruin your whole day."

They moved farther down the hall to the back of the house and found a closed door. "This must be his office," Margo said, opening the door slowly.

Sure enough, the small room held a chair and desk surrounded by tall stacks of bookcases that were crammed full of everything from paperback books, to CDs, to even some old VHS tapes. Mary walked over and picked one of the tapes up.

"Stanley still has a box of those, too," Rosie said. "He keeps saying they're coming back."

"Yeah, just like rotary dial phones," Margo said. She looked around the room. "So where do we start? Checking behind the stacks of books? Rifling through the desk drawers? Tapping on the walls for hidden panels?"

"Well, we could look on his computer," Mary suggested.

"Oh, yeah, good idea," Margo conceded.

Mary sat down on the chair and started up the computer. The screen appeared with a request for a password. "Well, crap, we need a password," she said in frustration.

"Oh, no problem," Margo said.

"What do you mean?" Mary asked. "We have no idea what his…"

Mary paused when Margo reached over and pulled a sticky note from the wall next to the computer and handed it to her. "Try this," Margo said.

Mary shook her head in disbelief. "But, he wouldn't have his password right next to his computer," Mary said, typing in the letters and numbers on the page anyway. She pressed the "Enter" key, and the system accepted the password and allowed her access to all the files.

"Why would he do that?" she asked incredulously.

"Because, like the rest of us, he can't remember his password," Margo said with a smile. "So, he keeps it right next to his computer."

"But…but…but…," Mary stammered.

"Don't try to make sense of it," Margo advised. "It is what it is."

Still shaking her head, Mary opened up his browser to check his browsing history. "Well, isn't this interesting?" she said.

"What is that?" Rosie asked.

"His browsing history," Mary replied. "It tracks all of the web pages he's visited in the past."

"Does every computer do that?" Rosie asked.

Mary nodded and smiled. "Unless you turn off the history area," she said.

"Why, that's simply amazing," Rosie said. "Who would have thought a computer could do that?"

"Anyway, it turns out that our friend Butch accessed articles on how to cut brake lines," Mary said. "And he also accessed schematics of the kind of car the Kochs drove."

"Let me see," Margo said, leaning over Mary and looking at the monitor. She pulled on her reading glasses and looked even closer. "And look at that. The dates are just before the Kochs were killed."

"I knew it," Margo said, straightening up. "I knew he did it."

"The question is," Mary said, "how do we prove it?"

Chapter Forty-one

Margo shook her head. "Well, if they could convict people for what they were searching for on their computers, my daughter, Ann, would be in a maximum security prison," she said. "Mystery writers have to look up all kinds of interesting things."

Mary nodded. "And even if we found the tools he used to cut the brake lines," she added, "there is no way we could prove that he used those tools for that purpose."

Rosie shrugged. "So we have to get him to confess," she said simply.

Margo and Mary turned and stared at their friend. "You make it sound like it's easy," Margo said.

"Well, it's not easy," Rosie agreed. "But, really, he's not that smart, and besides, he's messy. We should be able to figure out a way to get him to confess."

"A séance," Margo said.

Mary shook her head immediately. "Oh, no, I don't do séances," she said emphatically.

"I don't mean a real séance," Margo replied. "I mean a set up. So we scare Butch into confessing what he did."

Rosie clapped her hands. "Oh, that's a great idea," she said. "We can have it at my house." She paused for a moment and then looked at her friends. "What does one serve at a séance?"

"Hollow weenies?" Mary suggested.

Margo started to laugh when they heard the front door jiggle.

"Crap," Mary whispered, her heart thumping in her chest. "They're back."

Rosie shook her head. "They can't be back. We're still here."

"We need to hide," Margo said. She looked around the room and then looked down at Mary. "We need a fairly large hiding place."

"There's a pantry, between here and the kitchen," Rosie said. "It's a mess, but it's big enough."

"Let's go," Mary said, shutting down the computer and pushing herself out of the chair.

They quietly let themselves out of the office, closing the door softly behind them. The could hear the thumping sound of Butch's walker being guided into the front hall.

"Really, Butch," they heard Stanley say from the front of the house. "It's my treat. You don't need your wallet."

"No, I can't do that to you, Stanley," Butch replied from what sounded like the living room. "I know it's around here somewhere."

"Hurry," Rosie whispered, motioning them forward as she opened a narrow door in the hallway.

They tiptoed quickly and stuffed themselves into the long, narrow pantry. "It looked bigger when it was empty," Rosie said.

"I might have left it in the kitchen," Butch called.

"He'll never find it in there," Mary whispered.

Suddenly Rosie started to silently shake. Concerned, Mary placed her hand on her friend's shoulder. "Rosie," she whispered urgently. "Are you okay?"

Rosie turned, tears streaming down her cheeks, and she nodded as she wiped the moisture away. "I just got it," she whispered back, her voice hitching with emotion.

"Got what?" Mary asked.

"Hollow weenies," she said, clapping her hands over her mouth as she exploded with silent mirth.

Margo looked at Rosie, then Mary, and then turned away from both of them, her shoulders also shaking in noiseless amusement. "Stop it," Mary whispered urgently. "Both of you. This is—"

Hiccup. Hiccup. Hiccup

Both women turned at the same time and stared at Mary. They could hear Butch's footsteps right outside the pantry door. Mary shook her head and pointed down at her abdomen.

Hiccup. Hiccup. Hiccup.

The hiccups were internal, so they weren't causing any noise. But because of the close proximity in the closet, both of the other women could feel them. Both women's eyes were filled with nervous hysteria, and their bodies were shaking with laughter.

"I have to pee," Rosie breathed softly, which caused another bout of shaking and crying.

Mary was at her wit's end. She didn't want to think about the image they would present if Butch opened the pantry door—three women crammed into a tiny space, laughing hysterically.

The laughter halted immediately when they felt the movement of the doorknob.

Fear replaced mirth, and the women held their breath.

"Hey, Butch," Stanley called from the living room. "I found it."

"That's great," Butch replied, releasing the doorknob. "Thanks Stanley. Let's go eat."

They held their breath until they heard the front door close, and then they collapsed against the shelves.

"Let's drive to McDonalds," Rosie said, her voice shaking.

"McDonalds?" Mary asked.

Rosie nodded. "There is no way I'm going to use that man's bathroom," she replied. "Disgusting."

They giggled all the way to the car.

Chapter Forty-two

Mary climbed the steps to the second floor of the Freeport City Hall Building to Bradley's office. She hated that she was out of breath before she reached the top stair. Pausing for a moment to catch her breath, she leaned against the wall and took a deep breath before stepping out into the hall.

Dorothy, Bradley's administrative assistant, was behind the tall desk at the end of the hall. She looked up when she heard Mary enter the hall.

"Hi, Mary," she said with a smile. "Hasn't that baby been born yet?"

Mary smiled on the outside and grimaced on the inside. If one more person asked her that again, she might scream. "Nope," she said aloud, patting her belly. "He's still in there."

"Well, you look like you're ready to burst," she said.

Thank you, Mary thought, thank you very much.

But she smiled and shook her head. "No, not for a couple more months," she replied. "Is Bradley free for a few minutes?"

Dorothy nodded. "Yes, go on in," she said.

"Thanks," Mary said, walking passed Dorothy and knocking lightly on Bradley's door.

"Come in," she heard him call.

She opened the door and slipped inside his office. "Hi," she said when Bradley looked up.

His surprised smile lightened her heart, and when he stood up and came over to her, that same heart did a little flip-flop seeing him in his uniform.

"What a nice surprise," he said, leaning down and kissing her lightly on the lips. Then he paused. "This is a surprise, right? I wasn't supposed to meet you and I forgot?"

She grinned and shook her head. "No, this is a surprise," she said. "Do you have a few minutes to talk?"

"For you, anything," he said, leading her back to his desk.

He guided her to a chair and sat down next to her, rather than take his place on the other side of the desk. "So, what's up?" he asked.

She took a deep breath and then turned to him. "Well, remember last night when you asked me if I was trying to avoid your questions?" she asked.

"Which you obviously were," he pointed out.

She nodded affirmatively and took another deep breath.

"Any more deep breaths like that and I'm going to have to open the window to get more air in here," he teased.

"So, yesterday, Margo and Rosie thought they found some suspects in the Koch murder case," she explained. "Stanley didn't think so, but Margo actually had lunch with one guy and felt like he turned really defensive when they talked about the Kochs. Then she had ice cream with another guy and thought he went kind of psycho when they were talking about Frasier."

Bradley nodded, but said nothing.

She was about to take another deep breath, but stopped herself.

"We knew we had to get some evidence…" she began.

"I'm not going to like this, right?" he asked.

She shook her head. "No, you're not," she said. "We went to the first guy's house. Margo was actually able to get a neighbor to let her in, so it wasn't really breaking in. But, really, we don't think he's a suspect anymore."

"Well, that's a relief," Bradley said.

"You're being sarcastic, right?" Mary asked.

Bradley nodded. "Continue," he suggested.

"Okay, well, while Stanley took the second guy out for lunch, we went into his house to search it."

"You do understand that's breaking and entering," he said, his voice tight.

"Well, the door was unlocked, so we didn't have to break," she said quickly. "And he told Rosie she could drop by any time, so it wasn't exactly entering."

He stared at her for a long moment. "Rosie made that up, right?"

She nodded again.

He closed his eyes and shook his head. "Okay, what else?"

"We looked on his computer and found that he'd been researching how to cut brake lines and the schematic of the Koch's car just before they had their accident," she said quickly.

"So, he probably did do it," Bradley said.

"But we also know everything is circumstantial, and even though the car hasn't been destroyed, the evidence of a bad brake line probably is gone. No one actually thinks a crime was committed," she said.

"I'm not going to like this either, right?" he asked.

This time she smiled and shook her head. "Actually, it's not as bad as the first thing," she said.

"What?" he asked.

"We want to do a séance," she said, and before he could disagree she added, "Not a real séance. A fake one. But the Kochs will be there giving me information. We want to scare Butch into confessing. And, we could invite Eddie and see if he confesses, too."

"Kind of like a party," he said.

"You're being sarcastic again, right?"

He nodded slowly. "And you want to sit across the table from a murderer and pressure him until he snaps," he said. "Right?"

"Well, when you put it that way, it doesn't sound nearly as good as I want to wear a wire and I want you in the other room waiting to hear his confession," she said.

"Whose house?" he asked.

"Rosie and Stanley's," Mary replied.

"When?"

"Tonight," she said.

"Why tonight?" he asked.

"Because Margo is a huge part of this, and she has to leave tomorrow," Mary said. "Margo is the one who told Butch that the Kochs were her friends."

He sighed slowly and nodded. "Okay, tell them to invite him over at seven," he said. "We should get there by six and set things up."

"Thank you," she replied.

"You just have to promise me one thing," he said.

She nodded.

"Don't do anything that will put you or Mikey in jeopardy, okay?"

"Okay," she said. "I won't."

"And if I think things are headed in the wrong direction, I have full veto power over the entire thing," he said.

She nodded. "That's fair."

He sighed. "Okay, let the Brennans know we might not be able to come by tonight."

"I will," she said, pushing herself out of the chair. "Thank you."

He stood and pulled her into his arms. "You're going to drive me crazy," he said, kissing her.

"But you'll never be bored," she whispered, kissing him back.

"No," he said against her lips. "I'll never be bored."

Chapter Forty-three

Shivering, Mary let herself into the empty house and hurried to the thermostat to turn it up. The temperature was dropping rapidly, and the forecaster was predicting record-breaking temperatures before the end of the day. Slipping off her coat, she hung it up and then walked into the middle of her living room. She needed to get in touch with the Kochs so they would know about the fake séance, and she hoped they would respond to her calling out—the way they did last time.

"Hello," she called. "Hello. Can you hear me?"

She waited for a moment, looking around the room, and then she tried again. "Hello. I need to talk to you."

"I'm here."

Mary's heart dropped. She slowly turned around to face Julie.

"Hello Julie," Mary said.

The ghost glided across the room to stand directly in front of Mary. "I don't like you," she said.

Mary shook her head. "You don't know me," she replied.

"You're like those other girls who steal boyfriends," she said.

Mary shook her head. "No, that's not me," she said. "I was one of those girls who didn't have a boyfriend because I had three big brothers."

Julie studied her. "Do you know what it's like to be me?" she asked, her voice brittle. "Do you know what it's like to wait for your destiny?"

"Julie, listen…" Mary began.

"No!" Julie shouted. "You listen to me. He's mine."

A cold wind whipped through the house and knocked Mary backwards. She stumbled but caught herself before she fell. "Stop it," she yelled back.

The wind blew again, pushing Mary across the room. She grabbed hold of the back of a chair, but the next gale ripped her away from the furniture towards the kitchen. She grabbed for the counter, but she was being pummeled over and over again with freezing cold winds. Her fingers were numb, and she was shivering. "Julie, stop," she cried. "Please stop!"

The basement door flew open, and Mary felt a panic unlike she'd ever felt before. "Please, Julie, don't do this," she cried. "Please don't hurt my baby."

The force of the wind increased. Mary's hair blew in her face, blinding her. She wrapped her arms around the pillar that stood between the countertop and the cabinet. "No," she screamed. "Mike help me!"

She was slipping, and there was nothing she could do. "Please God," she prayed. "Please help me."

Digging her fingers into the wood, she tried to hold on. She felt another burst of wind, and she wrapped her arms more tightly around the pillar, holding on for dear life. The sub-zero temperatures made her skin burn, and the wind felt like sandpaper against her face. The wind hit again, and she heard the crack of the wood of the pillar give way. "No," she cried, desperately searching for something else to hold onto. "No, please."

An enormous blast of frigid wind ripped the pillar from its moorings, and Mary flew across the room. Knowing she was going to hit the wall, she was able to pivot so her back took the impact of the wall.

The impact knocked the breath out of her, and she fell to the ground, gasping. Then, suddenly, she was sliding across the floor towards the open basement door. She pushed her hands out in front of her to stop, but her hands were too numb and the pressure too great.

"No!" she screamed.

The basement stairs loomed dark and steep. She closed her eyes and screamed as the wind swept her through the doorway. She waited for the first hit, tensed for it, but nothing came. She opened her eyes and cried in relief when she saw Mike.

"I got you babe," Mike said as he enveloped her in his arms and carried her down the stairs, laying her on a piece of old carpet near the furnace.

Shivering and crying, her teeth rattling, she couldn't speak. "My…my…my…" she stammered.

"He's fine," Mike said to her. "Mikey's fine."

Tears of relief coursed down her cheeks, and exhausted, she collapsed against the carpet, her body still shaking from the cold.

"Come on, sweetheart," Mike said. "You can't sleep. You need to get warm."

"So…so…cold," she stammered, her eyes drifting closed.

Mike looked down at her and shook his head. "Forget the rules," he whispered.

He knelt down, picked her back up into his arms and whispered something Mary was too far gone to understand.

The fog started to clear. The cold began to thaw, and Mary almost immediately began to feel warmer, as if the heat was surrounding her from both the inside and the outside. Her shivering stopped. The fear was gone, being replaced by an overwhelming feeling of well-being and peace. She opened her eyes in wonder. "What?"

"God's warmth," Mike whispered.

"I feel amazing," she said.

He smiled down at her. "Yeah, it does that," he said.

He gently placed her on her feet. "Can you stand on your own?"

She stood and did a quick assessment. "I can not only stand," she said. "I feel like I could run a marathon."

He wrapped his arms around her and just held her for a moment. "I'm so sorry," he said.

"What? Why?" she asked.

"I brought her here," he said. "I asked you to go to the reunion. I didn't come when you called."

"But you came when I needed you," Mary insisted. "You came and you saved me. You're not responsible for her actions."

He stepped away from her. "She could have killed you," he said. "She doesn't deserve your help. I'm sending her away."

He started to move away, and she placed her hand on his shoulder, stopping him. "How did that happen?" she asked, knowing that her hand should have gone through him.

He shrugged. "A little residual effect from the warmth," he said.

"Okay, listen to me," she said. "I don't like what she did. I don't know why she's filled with hate. But, I'm not going to let her choices affect me. I'm not going to hate. I'm not going to be angry. I'm not going to stop being who I am and doing what I do. I won't let her change me."

"But Mary," he started to argue. "Once Bradley—"

"Oh, no," she said. "Bradley will not find out about this."

"Mary," Mike said.

"Mike," she interrupted. "This is our secret. At least for now. Okay? Please?"

With a frustrated sigh, he nodded. "Okay," he said. "For now. So, what's next?"

"We go upstairs," she said.

"But she's still up there," Mike said.

Mary took a deep breath and smiled. "For some reason, I feel like I can handle her this time."

Chapter Forty-four

Mary climbed up the stairs and stepped into the kitchen. She looked around and saw Julie standing on the other side of the counter. The ghost's eyes glossed over, and she waved her arms to generate more wind. But Mary turned to her and shook her head. "No," she said, lifting her arms defensively. "Not this time."

Suddenly, the ghost flew backwards, a shocked look on her face. "What did you do?" she screamed.

Mary looked down at her hands and then over at the ghost. "Just this," she said, repeating the same defensive gesture. Pure energy flowed from Mary's hands, knocking the ghost across the room. Mary grinned. "I really like residual effects," she said quietly.

For the first time since Mary met her, Julie actually looked frightened. A remnant of a young, frightened girl manifested itself. "Please don't hurt me," she pleaded. "I'm sorry. I won't try and hurt you again."

Mary studied her for a moment and realized this show of strength was the one thing that had finally reached her. Well, she wasn't going to back down now.

"I've been patient with you for as long as I can," Mary said firmly. "But now it's time to show you that I mean business. Do you understand?"

Julie nodded quickly. "Yes. Yes, I understand."

"Good. Now, I want you to be back here tomorrow night," Mary said. "If you come tomorrow, you won't have to worry about me hurting you. Is that a deal?"

Julie nodded. "Yes, it's a deal," she said.

"Don't make me come and find you," Mary threatened easily.

"No! No, I'll be back here," Julie promised anxiously.

"You can go now," Mary said and was delighted when the ghost faded away at her request.

Mike appeared next to her. "You handled that well," he said.

Mary looked down at her hands and then up at Mike. "Am I like an X-Man now?" she asked. "Do I have mutant powers?"

He chuckled despite himself and shook his head. "No, I can assure you this is just temporary," he said.

She grinned. "How long is temporary?" she asked.

"Mary," he said, trying to be serious. "Don't get carried away."

She shook her head. "No, of course not," she said. "Me? Get carried away? That would never happen."

She paused, considered the powers for a moment, and then looked at him. "Can I levitate things?"

"Mary," he warned.

She smiled. "Just kidding," she said. "But I do need to invite Eddie to the fake séance tonight. Do you think you could track down Frasier and Shirley and make sure they attend?"

"Yeah, I can do that," he said. "Are you sure you're okay?"

She smiled at him and nodded. "Really, I haven't felt this good for a long time," she said. "And I really hope when this wears off I don't suddenly feel everything it's been masking."

He shook his head. "It doesn't mask anything," he said. "It heals. It won't just wear off; the effects will just slowly dissipate."

She placed her hand on his shoulder, delighted she could still feel him. "I don't know if I thanked you," she said. "I have a feeling what you did went a little above and beyond your usual duties."

He smiled and shrugged. "Sometimes you gotta do what you gotta do."

"I am more grateful than you could know for what you did," she replied seriously. "I know you saved Mikey and me."

He placed his hand over hers, and she could feel the power inside her intensify. "We're family," he said. "Sometimes you're born into a family and sometimes you get adopted into one. I'm grateful to be part of yours."

"Same here," she said.

He released her hand and stepped back. "Okay, I'll go find Shirley and Frasier," he said. "And I'll be at the séance, too."

"Thanks, Mike," she said. "For everything."

Chapter Forty-five

She drove over to Eddie's shop, occasionally glancing down at the clock as she went. It was nearly closing time, and she wanted to be sure and catch him before he went home. As luck would have it, he was just locking the door when Mary pulled up in front of his business.

"Eddie. Hi," she called as she pushed herself out of her car. "I'm Mary O'Reilly. We met a couple of days ago."

He nodded. "Yeah, I remember you," he said. "How are you doing?"

"Great," she said with a smile. "I'm great. But I've had some developments on your parents' case."

His smile dropped, and he shook his head. "I really don't think they were murdered," he said. "Dad was upset. He was probably driving too fast for conditions. That's all it was. People just die sometimes; it doesn't have to be a big mystery."

"Actually, I know they were murdered," she said. "And I really need your help to discover who the murderer is."

He shook his head. "I don't know," he said. "I've got a lot of work to do. And I don't think I'd be of much help."

"I really need you," Mary said. "Tonight."

He put his keys in his pocket and started walking towards his car. "Tonight? What's tonight?"

"We're, um, we're having a séance," she said.

He stared at her for a moment. "Are you kidding me?" he asked. "What kind of crazy, woo-woo operation do you have? A séance?"

"We feel it's the only way your parents will be able to let us know about their murderer," she said. "I really don't like to resort to séances, but this time it is the right thing to do."

"Yeah, well, no thanks," he said adamantly. "You can count me out. This is just crazy and, quite frankly, not something either of my parents would have wanted to do."

Mary nodded. "I understand that," she argued. "But it's really important…"

Reaching his car, he unlocked it remotely and opened the door. "Sorry," he said. "But my answer is final and it's no."

Mary reached out and placed her hand on his shoulder to stop him from getting into the car. "But…"

She stopped when she saw the surprised look on his face and a change come over him. He took a deep breath and smiled at her. "When did you want me to be there?" he asked.

"At seven," she said, pulling a notecard out of her pocket. "And here's the address."

He glanced down at the card and smiled. "Yeah, I know where this is," he said, nodding. "Okay, I'll see you in a couple of hours."

He slipped into his car, turned it on and drove away. Mary stood at the curb for a moment, watching his car drive down the block. Once he was out of sight, she looked down at her hands again, turned them over and shook her head in awe. Then she grinned and lifted one hand up and made a slight sweeping motion. "These aren't the droids you're looking for."

She chuckled and took a deep breath. "This is awesome."

Chapter Forty-six

"This has never happened to me before," Bradley said as he repositioned Mary's wire again. "I'm getting nothing but static."

"Maybe it's a pregnancy thing?" Mary suggested.

"Yeah, or maybe it's your special powers," Bradley said, shaking his head.

"What do you mean?" Mary asked, surprised.

"You know," Bradley said. "Your ability to see ghosts. Maybe those psychic abilities mess up electronic frequencies?"

She sighed with relief and nodded. "Yeah, that makes sense," she said. "How about if we wire Stanley?"

"What are you talking about girlie?" Stanley asked. "I ain't never had nothing like that on me."

Bradley walked over to Stanley with the tiny wireless mike. "It's no big deal," he said. "I just tape this tiny microphone under your clothes, and then it picks up the sounds in the room," Bradley said. "So, when I'm in the other room, I can hear what's going on in here."

Stanley looked skeptically down at the small device. "Can it electrocute me?" he asked.

Bradley rolled his eyes. "Of course it can, Stanley," he said. "Which is why I was just trying to tape it to my pregnant wife."

Grumbling, Stanley started unbuttoning his shirt. "Well, there's no need to have an attitude about it," he muttered.

Mary clapped her hand over her mouth to hold back her laughter and walked to where Rosie and Margo were laying out the refreshments for the post-séance party.

"You know," Mary said. "If we actually catch the murderer tonight, there might not be a party."

Rosie smiled at her. "Oh, that's okay dear," she said. "We made extra in case there are lots of police officers here."

"And we're using paper cups and plates in case there's a fire fight and they have to up end the table for a barrier," Margo said, equally as nonchalantly as Rosie.

"Okay, then," Mary replied. "I guess you have it all covered."

Margo smiled at Mary and then gently patted her cheek. "Murder is my business dear," she said.

Mary enveloped Margo in a hug. "You are simply amazing," she said. "I'm so glad you came here to recuperate."

Margo looked up at Mary with a strange look on her face. Then she stepped away.

"What?" Mary asked. "Did I do something?"

Margo shook her head and then took a couple of steps in a circle. "My hip," she said slowly, taking a few more steps. "My hip suddenly feels good. No, not good. Great."

"Margo, I'm so happy for you," Rosie replied. "See, I told you that yak ointment I gave you would do the trick."

"You still have that yak ointment?" Mary asked, remembering when Rosie tried to give it to her.

Rosie shrugged. "Well, it was non-refundable," she explained. "But look. It's worked miracles."

Margo looked from Rosie to Mary and then back to Rosie again. "Yes," she said slowly. "That must be it."

Rosie grinned. "I'm so delighted it worked," she replied, patting the table happily. "Okay, we still need napkins."

Once Rosie had left the room, Margo turned to Mary and shook her head. "It wasn't the yak ointment," she said quietly.

"I know," Mary replied. "I would have been able to smell that on you a mile away."

Giggling softly, Margo nodded. "Yes, I opened the jar, immediately closed it and had to air out my bedroom for an hour," she agreed.

"Well, whatever it was that healed you," Mary said, "I'm so glad you're feeling better."

"Thank you, Mary," Margo replied. "And now, let's go catch a murderer."

Chapter Forty-seven

With Bradley safely ensconced in headphones in the guest room with a plate of cookies, several sandwiches, a pitcher of water, a linen tablecloth and napkins all provided by Rosie, they were ready to get started. At five minutes before seven, the front doorbell rang, and Rosie turned to Mary, her eyes wide with apprehension.

"What should I do?" she asked.

"Answer the door," Mary prompted gently.

Rosie giggled nervously. "Well, of course," she replied.

Stanley accompanied Rosie to the door, and they opened it to find Eddie standing on the porch.

"Hi," he said hesitantly. "I'm Eddie Koch. My parents..."

"Of course," Rosie said. "We loved your parents. Please come in. My name is Rosie Wagner, and this is my husband, Stanley."

As Eddie entered the house, Stanley walked over and thrust his chest as close to Eddie as he could get it. "What's your name again?" Stanley asked. "I don't know if I heard it correctly."

Eddie stepped back, but Stanley followed. "It's Eddie," he stammered. "Eddie Koch."

Stanley nodded. "Yeah, I got that this time," he said, and then he raised his voice. "That was Eddie. Eddie Koch."

Mary closed her eyes for a brief moment, praying for patience, and then she joined them at the door. "Eddie, I'm so glad you could make it," she said. "Why don't you come on over to the table and have a seat. We're going to begin in a moment. Margo, I don't think you've met Eddie yet."

Margo greeted the young man and diplomatically guided him away from Stanley and towards the large dining room table where the séance was going to be held.

"Stanley," Mary whispered fiercely when Eddie was across the room.

"You think Bradley heard that?" he asked.

"I think Bradley is going to be deaf for a week," she replied. "The microphone is very sensitive. You don't have to get that close to people in order to have it pick up their voices. It's built to be discreet."

"Well, then why didn't anyone tell me?" he asked. "Here I was thrusting my chest out like a darn, fool rooster."

"I'm sorry," she said. "We should have told you. Now…"

She was interrupted by another doorbell ring. "That will be Butch," she said.

Stanley nodded. "Don't worry, girlie," he said. "I got it covered now."

He walked over to the door and greeted Butch, guiding him slowly to the table because of his walker. Margo walked over to Mary and shook her head. "I was so overwhelmed with his comments at the ice cream parlor that I forgot about his walker," she whispered. "How in the world could he cut brake lines when he can barely get around?"

Mary shook her head. "I don't know," she whispered back. "But at this point, all we can do is see what happens."

Both of the women joined the others around the table. Mary sat at the head of the table and nodded to Stanley, who turned off the lights, so only a candle in the middle of the table lit the room.

"Thank you all for coming tonight," Mary said. "I know this is unusual. But we wanted to see if we could speak to Frasier and Shirley one last time to determine the details of their deaths."

Butch shifted in his chair. "I'm actually an agnostic when it comes to this kind of crap," he said loudly. "Maybe I shouldn't be here. Wouldn't want to chase the spirits away."

"Oh, I think you're fine," Rosie said. "I think Frasier and Shirley were Republicans, but they had open minds."

Margo, seated on the other side of Butch, muffled a chuckle. "I think it's important that our combined energies help summon them," Margo added. "So, really Butch, the more the merrier."

"Could we just get on with it?" Eddie asked.

"Of course," Mary said. She took a deep breath and closed her eyes. "Shirley and Frasier, we ask you to come forth from the abyss and meet with us, your friends and family."

"We weren't in no abyss," Frasier said, standing alongside Mary. "We were in the kitchen waiting. Can't these people ever shut up?"

"Hush, Frasier," Shirley said, slapping her husband's arm. "These things take time."

"How would you know?" he asked. "How many séances have you been to?"

Shirley just huffed in response.

Mary was grateful that no else could hear the ghosts. She calmly took another breath. "I can feel their spirits in the room with us."

Eddie looked around the room, his eyes glistening with tears. "Mom. Dad," he said. "I'm so sorry."

Chapter Forty-eight

Shirley moved around the table and stood next to her son, placing her hand on his shoulder. Eddie's eyes widened, and he looked at Mary. "I can feel her," he said. "I can feel my mom."

"Hogwash," Butch mumbled.

"Could you repeat that?" Stanley asked, leaning over towards Butch.

"I said hogwash," Butch repeated.

"Thank you," Stanley replied.

But Eddie wasn't paying attention to them. "I'm so sorry," he said softly.

"They want to know why you're sorry," Mary said.

"Yeah, did he kill us?" Frasier asked. "But, I'm telling you, a simple I'm sorry isn't going to do it."

Eddie took a deep breath. "I'm sorry I wasn't the son you wanted," he said. "I'm sorry I kept giving up on things when I just should have worked through them. I'm sorry we argued…"

He choked back a sob. "I'm so sorry we argued on that last night," he said. "If there were any way I could take those words back."

"Your father has a question for you," Mary said.

"I do?" Frasier asked.

"He wants to know why you haven't destroyed the car," Mary continued. "Why you kept it hidden at the junk yard."

Eddie shook his head and sighed. "I thought they'd understand," he said. "I thought, you know, it would make it better, at least in a small way."

He turned to Mary. "When you spoke to me, I realized that the insurance company, or whoever you are working for, would find out about the car," he said. "I couldn't have their investigators searching the car. I couldn't have them find…"

He stopped talking and sighed. Then he reached his hand inside his jacket. "I brought this, because I knew all the questions needed to stop," he said.

Mary held her breath, expecting Eddie to pull a gun out on them.

"Eddie wait," she said. "This isn't—"

"No, I have to do it," he said. "It's important."

He pulled out his fisted hand, held it out over the table and then opened it. A soft "ping" sounded.

"That was a soft ping," Stanley said. "Iffen anyone listening couldn't hear it."

"What? What is it?" Mary asked.

"Oh," Shirley gasped. "My earring. My pearl earring."

"An earring?" Mary said. "Your mom's pearl earring."

Eddie quickly glanced at Mary. "She really is here, isn't she?" he asked, amazed.

Mary nodded.

"Mom," Eddie said. "They couldn't find your earring. They said it must have been lost at the crash site. I know how much you loved them…"

"Eddie bought them for me when he got his first job." She lifted her hand up and moved her hair, and Mary saw that indeed, she was only wearing one earring. "They meant so much to me."

"I couldn't let them destroy the car," he said. "I had to find it."

Frasier wiped the tears from his cheeks. "That's my son," he said, his voice hoarse. "That's the Eddie I have always been proud of."

"You bought them for her," Mary said. "When you got your first job."

Eddie nodded. "Every time she wore them, it helped me remember the person I could be," he said. "I never felt I failed her. Only my dad."

Mary glanced over at Frasier. He nodded and glided around the table to where his son was seated and placed his hand on Eddie's other shoulder. Eddie gasped. "He's here, too," he said, looking at Mary for confirmation.

She nodded. "Yeah, he's been here the whole time."

"I'm so sorry, Dad," Eddie said.

"No, I'm the one who's sorry," Frasier interrupted. "I never gave you a chance."

"He said he's the one who's sorry," Mary said. "He feels that he never gave you a chance."

"No, Dad, you gave me a lot of chances. I just blew them," Eddie replied.

"You shouldn't limit the number of chances you give people," Frasier said. "You should love them and encourage them, no matter what."

Mary repeated Frasier's words, and Eddie shook his head, chuckling softly through his tears. "But then we wouldn't have had anything to talk about," he whispered.

Frasier laughed sadly and nodded. "That was my fault, too," he said, shaking his head with regret.

"He said that was his fault, too," Mary said. "He's so sorry."

"I think we were both at fault," Eddie said. "I love you, Dad."

"I love you too, son," Frasier said softly.

Eddie looked over at Mary and smiled through his tears. "You don't have to repeat it," he said, his voice cracking. "I heard him. I heard him loud and clear."

"I'm not falling for this crap," Butch suddenly shouted. "They are dead. They are gone. There's no one here in this room except us."

Chapter Forty-nine

The room was shrouded in instant silence, and everyone stared at Butch.

"Why the hell is he here?" Frasier asked, finally noticing the other people around the table. "He's supposed to be in jail."

Mary looked over at Butch. "You're supposed to be in jail?" she asked.

He shook his head. "No, the case was thrown out," he said.

"Well, damn, of course," Frasier said. "I missed that court date, didn't I?"

"What court date?" Mary asked.

"The court date I was supposed to have the week after the accident," Frasier replied. He turned to Shirley. "I've been such an idiot. I was so focused on the argument with Eddie, I didn't even think about the embezzlement."

"Embezzlement?" Mary repeated, feeling like she just walked into a parallel universe.

"You heard that, right?" Stanley shouted. "She said embezzlement."

Butch stood up and slid his chair back.

"Oh, look," Rosie said. "He can walk without his walker. It's a miracle."

Margo looked across to her friend. "I would guess that the walker is a ruse," she said. "So people wouldn't consider him for the crimes he committed."

Butch turned to Margo. "There's no evidence," he said. "The only eyewitness died before he could testify. Besides, it was all the musings of an angry, jealous, disturbed man."

"What is he talking about?" Shirley asked.

Frasier sighed. "I discovered that someone had been skimming money off the books at the VFW," he said. "Money that was supposed to go towards scholarships and widows."

She nodded. "I remember," she said. "You told me Melvin did it. You told me you confronted him and told him if he paid it back, you wouldn't go to the authorities."

"Melvin insisted he was innocent," he said. "But I didn't listen to him. I told him I had enough proof to send him away for a long time. So, he paid."

Mary looked at Butch. "You set Melvin up to take the fall?" she asked. "You stole the money and made Melvin the fall guy?"

Butch smiled. "I don't know what you're talking about," he said. "There is no evidence to the contrary. And the word of a ghost doesn't tend to stand up in court."

"The word of a ghost might not," Margo said. "But the word of an FBI agent might."

"What?" Butch exclaimed, turning towards Margo.

She shrugged. "I knew there was something suspicious about you when I first met you," she said. "Sharply honed intuition. And you weren't clever enough to clear the history on your computer."

"What?" he asked.

She nodded and repeated his password to him. "Electronic surveillance is quite remarkable."

His face turned ashen. "How much do you know?" he stammered.

"How much do you think I know?" she countered. "Shall we start with how-to articles on cutting car brakes, schematics of the Koch's car, or do you want me to start talking about your bank accounts?"

He started to glance nervously around the room.

"Don't even think about trying to get away," Margo added. "I have the place surrounded."

"I was desperate," he said. "I needed the money. I had just lost everything I had investing in currency. It wasn't that much. If only Frasier had let it go."

Margo pushed her chair back and faced him. "Say it," she said. "Before my guys break down these doors and haul you away, we all deserve to hear you say it."

Eddie stood up. "I deserve to hear it from you, too," he said.

"I cut the brake lines," he said. "I didn't mean to kill them. I just wanted to put him in the hospital for a while. Then I could get out of town. Really, I didn't mean to kill him."

"Did everyone hear that?" Stanley yelled at his chest.

"Yes, Stanley," Bradley said, walking into the room. "Everyone heard that."

"Butch Beck, you are under arrest for the murder of Shirley and Frasier Koch," Bradley said, coming forward and slipping his handcuffs out of his waistband.

He turned to Margo and smiled. "Thank you, Agent Taylor," he said. "Your cooperation in this case has been extremely helpful."

Chapter Fifty

"I didn't know you were an FBI agent," Rosie said once Butch had been led from the room.

"I'm not," Margo said.

"But you said…" Rosie began.

"I just said that the word of an FBI agent would be taken in court," she said with a quick shrug. "I wasn't lying. I never said it was me."

"But how did you know about his financial records?" Stanley asked.

"I didn't," Margo replied. "But I figured if he was ignorant enough to confess to the group of us about embezzling, he wasn't much smarter with his financial records."

"Margo, you saved the day," Mary said. "Thank you."

She shrugged. "I've learned a lot about bluffing from Ann's books," she replied, and then her face brightened. "I wonder if she'd be able to use this in a book." Then she sighed. "No. No one would ever believe it."

Mary nodded. "I know. My life can be fairly unbelievable," she said. "Stranger than fiction."

Stanley stood up, reached under his shirt and pulled out the microphone and tape. "Iffen you'll give this back to Bradley," he said, "I'll take Rosie and Margo out for ice cream, so they can spend the last night of their visit chatting like magpies and Eddie can have a few minutes with his parents."

Mary pushed herself out of her chair and took the microphone. "Thank you, Stanley," she said.

Walking over to Margo, she gave her a hug. "I loved getting to know you," Mary said. "Please come back and visit again."

Margo nodded. "And you have to come out and visit me in Deadwood," she said. "I promise I'll show you all around town."

"Deal," Mary said, and then she looked down at her belly. "But it won't be anytime soon."

Margo laughed. "Understood."

Rosie came over and gave Mary a hug. "Just lock the door after you," she said. "I'll call you tomorrow."

They left, and the room was quiet for a moment, with only Rosie's grandfather clock ticking in the background.

"Are they still here?" Eddie finally asked.

Mary nodded. "Yes, they are," she said.

"Tell him we love him," Shirley said.

"Your mom says she loves you."

He nodded. "I always knew that," he replied, his voice thick with emotion. He looked around the room. "I miss you, Mom. I miss calling you whenever I felt like it. I miss your laughter. I miss your smile."

Shirley nodded through her tears. "I miss you, too."

"She misses you, too," Mary said, wiping the tears from her own cheeks.

"Tell him I'm proud of him," Frasier asked. "Please?"

"Your dad says he's proud of you."

"Really?" Eddie asked, looking surprised. "Really?"

"Yeah, tell him that I've been an idiot," Frasier said. "And someday, when he's a dad, he needs to remember the mistakes I made and do things the right way."

Mary took a deep, shuddering breath. "He said that he's been an idiot, and you need to remember not to make those same mistakes when you're a dad."

Eddie laughed nervously. "I don't know if I'm ready to even think about becoming a dad," he said.

"You'd make a great dad," his mom replied.

"Your mom thinks you'd make a great dad."

He laughed. "She just wants grandkids," he said. Then he stopped. His smile crumpled and he sobbed. "She's never going to meet her grandkids."

"Sure she is," Mary assured him. "But she won't only get to be a grandmother, she'll get to be a guardian angel."

He wiped his cheeks and took a deep breath. "I love you," he said. "Both of you."

They both heard a soft ping and turned towards the table. A second pearl earring rolled over to lie by the first one.

"Tell him to give them to his wife," Shirley said. "A gift from me."

"She wants you to give them to your wife," Mary said. "As a gift from her."

He nodded. "I will," he said.

"Then she'll have both of my most precious gifts," Shirley said smiling down at her son.

"Your mom said that then your wife will have both of her most precious gifts," Mary said, trying hard not to sob.

"Just make sure she can cook," Frasier said.

Mary's laugh was watery. "Your dad wants you to be sure she can cook."

Eddie laughed, too, as he wiped his eyes. "If she can cook like Mom, I'll marry her on the spot," Eddie said.

"Smart boy," Frasier said. "Takes after his dad."

Shirley wrapped her arm around her husband's arm and leaned against him. "Yes. Yes he does."

She looked up and sighed. "Mary, I see the light," she said. "Tell Eddie we'll be watching over him."

"I will," Mary said.

She turned to Eddie. "It's time for them to move on."

"I love you," he said. "I'll make you proud, I promise."

"You already have," his dad said, but this time both Eddie and Mary heard his voice.

Mary watched them fade into the light. Then she turned to Eddie. "How are you doing?"

He took a deep breath. "I'm good, actually," he said. "I feel better today than I have in a long time." He looked over at the earrings and carefully picked them up. "I guess I better start looking for a wife."

Mary smiled. "I agree," she said. "I wouldn't put it past your parents to come back and haunt you."

He laughed and nodded. "Yeah, I agree," he said. "Thank you, Mary."

"You are very welcome," she replied.

Chapter Fifty-one

The fire was crackling in the fireplace, the lights were turned down low and Mary was snuggled up on the couch with a fleece throw tucked around her when Bradley arrived home.

"So, how did it go?" she asked, as he slipped out of his coat and hung it up in the closet.

"I called Alex Boettcher, the DA, and he's going to run over to Stanley's house tonight and get a statement from Margo before she leaves town," he said. "But, with the recorded confession and the amazing fact that the car had not been crushed, there shouldn't be a problem with a conviction."

He removed his revolver, put it in the gun safe on the closet's top shelf and then crossed over to her, slipping beside her on the couch. "How did it go for you?" he asked, putting his arm around her and pulling her close.

She sighed and cuddled against him. "It's always that mixed bag, you know," she said. "The case has been solved, the murderer found and the spirits get to cross over. But, then they have to cross over and to family members, it's like losing them all over again. Eddie was sweet, I was bawling like a baby and so were Frasier and Shirley."

She shifted and looked up at him. "But Shirley left him the sweetest gift," she said. "You know the pearl earring?"

Bradley smiled. "The one that made the soft ping that Stanley told me about?"

She laughed and nodded. "Yes, that one," she said. "Somehow Shirley was able to leave the other one. They were a gift from Eddie to Shirley and now they're going to be a gift from Shirley to Eddie's wife."

"He's getting married?" Bradley asked.

Mary cuddled back in beside him. "Not yet," she said. "But he's going to start looking. He's got a set of grandparents and guardian angels ready and waiting."

Bradley was silent for a moment and then he sighed softly. "I never thought of it that way," he said. "I never even considered that my parents might be watching over Clarissa."

Mary laid her head against his chest. "Well, considering how protected she was until we finally found her," she said. "It makes a lot of sense."

"Yeah, it does," he replied softly. "It really does."

They sat there in the darkened room with the fire softly crackling in comfortable silence for a few minutes. Finally, Bradley shifted slightly, propping his feet on the coffee table and pulling her even closer. "So, how was your afternoon?" he asked.

Well, crap, Mary thought, *I don't want to lie, but I really don't want to tell him about what happened. I wonder if I still have any residual power.*

She placed her hand on his arm. "You don't want to know about my afternoon," she said, in her best Obi-Wan impression.

"Yes I do," he replied, looking at her with curiosity. "What's going on."

Yeah, no residual power left, she decided.

"Well, the good news is, I'm fine," she began.

His propped feet came down from the table and he turned towards her. "Tell me," he demanded. "And don't leave anything out."

"Well, funny story," she said. "The last time I came home and was calling out, trying to get Julie to appear, Shirley and Frasier appeared. And this time, when I wanted to get Shirley and Frasier to appear..."

"Julie was here?" Bradley asked. "What did she do?"

"She was pretty upset," Mary said. "And she had this whole combination pack of Mr. Freeze and Storm from X-Men."

"And?"

"And she kind of threw me around the kitchen with freezing cold gale force winds," she said quickly. "But, I'm okay. Mike caught me when she threw me down the basement stairs."

"She threw…" he stood up and walked away from her, running his hand through his hair in frustration. Then he turned back to her. "And you were going to tell me this, when?"

"I didn't really have a specific plan," she admitted.

"Mary, how can I trust you?" he shouted.

She stood up and walked over to him. "Okay, wait just a minute," she replied. "I told you the truth when you asked me. Didn't I?"

He nodded. "Yes, you did," he said. "But only because I asked."

She folded her arms over her chest. "Last week the police department had a drug raid on an apartment building in Freeport," she said. "Shots were fired. Did any come close to you?"

Bradley opened his mouth and then shut it. "I was fine," he said.

"What?" she asked, not a little sarcastically. "You didn't immediately call me and tell me that you had nearly been shot?"

"Mary, it's my job," he said. "Besides, I was fine."

She raised one eyebrow and stared at him for a long moment.

He thought about what he just said and then shook his head. "Oh, I see what you just did there," he said. "But, no, it's different."

She tilted her head and waited.

"Because…" he thought about it for a moment. "I'm not pregnant."

She shook her head. "Nope."

"Because if something, anything, happened to you my world would be destroyed?" he asked.

"Charming. But no," she said. "Because I feel the same way about you."

He sighed and looped his arms around her waist and pulled her closer. "Because I'm a stupid man who thinks I should be able to control everything and protect the people I love," he said, lowering his forehead to hers. "And when I can't it makes me crazy."

She smiled up at him. "Better," she said. She reached up and kissed him.

"I admit I was frightened beyond belief," she said. "And for a few moments, I didn't know if I was going to make it. And, if it hadn't been for Mike, the outcome would have been a lot different."

He took a deep shuddering breath. "This isn't helping me," he said.

"Wait until you see the kitchen," she replied. "And, once again, there's no way we can explain it to the insurance company."

"I don't think I want you to do this anymore," he said. "Right now. Standing here. With you in my arms. I can tell you that I would do just about anything to have you stop helping ghosts."

She sighed. "It's what I do," she said. "And most of the time, it's amazing."

He nodded. "I know," he said. "But those other times scare the hell out of me." He kissed her again. "I'm not going to ask you to make any decisions, especially after the day you've had, but think about it, okay?"

She nodded. "Yeah, okay."

Chapter Fifty-two

Mary sat on the couch watching the glowing embers in the fireplace slowly fade to black. She'd tried to sleep, but the conversation she had with Bradley kept running through her mind. He'd never force her to stop helping spirits, but he'd asked. Wrapping her arms around her belly, she felt Mikey move and sighed. So much had changed in such a short amount of time. How did people deal with change like that? How did they adapt so everyone was happy? Satisfied?

"How are you doing?" Mike asked, appearing on the chair across from her.

She sighed, suddenly close to tears and shook her head. "I don't know," she confessed.

"What's up?" he asked.

"I told Bradley about this afternoon," she said, and then she shook her head. "Actually, I didn't go into a lot of detail, but he got the gist of it."

"And how did he react?"

"He was upset," she said. "Worried, frightened, frustrated. All those male emotions when they want to protect the people they love."

Mike smiled. "Yeah, that sounds about right."

"He wants me to quit," she said. "He wants me to stop being who I am, doing what I do."

Mike was silent for a moment. "What if this same scenario happened in six months, and Mikey was in a high chair in the kitchen?" he finally asked.

Mary felt sick to her stomach. "He could have been…" She couldn't say it. She just shook her head.

"Even if his high chair hadn't been thrown across the room," Mike said, not sparing her feelings. "What if he had been exposed to cold like that? How long would he have survived?"

"But this was an unusual case," Mary argued weakly. "This has never happened before."

"Does that guarantee it will never happen again?" he asked.

She stared into the darkening coals for several minutes. "But I agreed to do this," she said. "This is part of me. I don't want to have to close down this part of me."

Mike nodded. "Yeah, I get it," he said. "This gift you have, this part of you, fulfills you. It makes you feel like you're accomplishing amazing, miraculous things. You're making a difference."

"And I love it," she admitted. "I love figuring out mysteries. I love moving people on to the other side. I love helping families find each other."

Mike shook his head. "I never understood it until just now."

"What? What don't you understand?" she asked.

"How hard it is to be a woman," he said.

She smiled. "Mike, you're not a woman."

He chuckled softly. "No, you goose, how hard it is to be you," he said. "When men say they want it all, that usually consists of a good job, a wife, kids, and a couple of rounds of golf every week."

He looked at Mary. "But when women want it all, they can't have it," he continued. "If they want a family, they can either hire someone to raise their kids or give up their job. If they want a career, they have to give up having kids, or they have to juggle the responsibilities of being a mother and an employee. They feel pulled in so many directions. Someone has to lose. And it's usually them."

"And some of them don't have choices," Mary said. "They would love to be home with their kids, but they can't. I know so many women who live with constant guilt because they can't do all they really want to do."

"What do you want to do, Mary?" Mike asked.

"What will I have to give up, Mike?" she asked.

He smiled and shook his head. "I don't know."

"If I could compromise," she said. "I don't want it to go away. I want to help. But I don't want to jeopardize my family. Can I have both? Can I have it all?"

"Well, I would think if anyone could help you have it all, it would be your employer," he said with a smile. "Let me see what I can find out."

"Thank you," she replied. "By the way, the residual effect has worn off, at a very inconvenient time, if you ask me."

He grinned. "Maybe, maybe not," he said. "It can only be used for truth, justice and..."

"I know," she said. "The American way."

He shook his head. "Nope. God's way, Mary," he started to fade away. "Only God's way."

Chapter Fifty-three

The doorbell rang at precisely ten o'clock, and Mary hurried to answer it. Stanley and Rosie stood outside with cardboard boxes in their arms.

"I think I got everything you need," Rosie said. "But Stanley is going to have to run over to the party store and pick up the ball."

Stanley shook his head. "Are you sure you know what you're doing?" he asked. "Seems like a pretty havey-cavey scheme to me."

"Well, it's the best idea I have," Mary said. "So I'm hoping it works. Stanley, before you go to the party store, would you both help me down in the basement for a few minutes?"

Stanley rolled his eyes. "What, you got some spiders you need killing?" he asked.

Mary smiled. "No, but I need your big he-man muscles, because there are some boxes that need rearranging."

"Women, always rearranging stuff," he grumbled. "Why can't you just leave it where it is?"

The old locker box was in the far corner of the basement under several boxes of things from

Bradley's house that had never been unpacked. "I need to get to the chest," Mary said.

"What's in there?" Rosie asked.

"Things that belonged to Bradley's father," she said. "I'm hoping it will help me get rid of our unwanted visitor."

Stanley moved the boxes to the side, and Mary unlatched the wooden box. On top was the letterman sweater, slightly yellowed and wrapped in tissue paper. She pulled it out and hung it in the air. "What do you think?" she asked. "Will it fit Bradley?"

"It should," Rosie said, examining it carefully. "Yes, I believe it will."

Mary pulled out a few boxes and then came to a box with a collection of 45 rpm records. "Oh, look at these," she said, pulling the record and the sleeve out of the box. "Oh, I wish we could play these records tonight. That would be so great."

"Don't see why you can't," Stanley said.

"Well, because I don't have anything to play them on," Mary replied.

Stanley put his hands of his hips and shook his head. "And that is why, girlie, you don't throw perfectly good things away."

"What do you mean?" she asked.

"Well, in the back shelves of our basement I have a portable record player with attached speakers," he said.

"Are you kidding me?" Mary exclaimed. "And it still works?"

"Course it works," he grumbled. "Why in the world would I keep a broken one?"

"Could I borrow it for tonight?" Mary asked. "Pretty please."

Stanley smiled. "Course you can, girlie," he said. "I'll bring it over after I pick up the ball."

They carried several items from the locker upstairs, and then Stanley left while Rosie and Mary got things ready.

"I don't want you to do too much climbing," Rosie said. "You have to be careful in your condition."

Thinking back to the day before, she nodded and smiled. "I agree," she said.

"By the way," Rosie asked, looking from the dining room into the kitchen, "what in the world happened in there?"

"An angry ghost with a lot of power," Mary admitted.

Rosie turned and looked at Mary. "And you were home at the time?" she asked.

Mary nodded. "Yes, I think she was mostly angry at me."

"Have you ever considered doing something else?" Rosie asked. "Something less dangerous? Just while your children are small?"

Mary put the rolls of crepe paper on the table and turned to her friend. "How can I do that?" she asked. "I feel so responsible."

Rosie came over to Mary and took her hand. "Oh, sweetheart, you don't know anything about feeling responsible yet," she said. "You just wait until you hold little Mikey in your arms. That will change your whole perspective on the world."

"But I'm already a mom," Mary reasoned. "I have Clarissa."

"Well, yes, but Clarissa was already a fairly independent and smart as a whip youngster," Rosie said, "who needed love, attention and guidance, but that's nothing like having a newborn whose very survival depends on you."

"Do you think I'll change?" Mary asked.

"Call your mother and ask her," Rosie said with a smile. "She'll explain it to you."

Chapter Fifty-four

Several hours later, the living room had been transformed, and Rosie and Stanley were headed back to their own house for a well-deserved rest. Mary sat on the stairs and dialed her mother's phone number. A minute later her mom answered the phone.

"Mary, how are you feeling?" Margaret O'Reilly asked.

"I'm a little tired," Mary replied honestly. "But I feel good."

"Oh, well, darling, get used to feeling tired," her mother teased. "That will be with you for the next eighteen years."

Mary leaned back on the staircase, trying to get comfortable. "Is that true?" she asked. "Is my whole life going to change when Mikey is born?"

"Aye, it will," Margaret said. "Does that worry you?"

"I don't know," Mary said. "I guess I really wasn't thinking about it. I mean, I obviously know I'm pregnant. I know that Mikey is going to be born in a few months. I know I'll have a baby. But the rest, I don't know, it's almost like it's not real."

Margaret chuckled. "Yes. That's exactly right," she said. "You've never experienced something like this, so how could you possibly imagine what it's going to be like?"

Mary shook her head. "But I've taken care of Clarissa," Mary said.

"Yes, and you've been a wonderful mother to her," her mother said gently. "And she loves you and trusts you. I'm so proud of you."

"But," Mary encouraged.

Her mother laughed. "But," she said. "This experience, of giving birth, of having a wee babe placed in your arms, of holding him and bonding with him. There is nothing that can prepare you for the change you'll experience, the love you immediately feel for this tiny, wrinkled newborn. It's a miracle in itself."

"Rosie said I'll change," Mary said. "That the things I want now won't be what I'll want then."

"Darling, love changes people," she explained. "It makes you want different things because there are more pieces to the puzzle. How about an experiment?"

Mary nodded. "Okay."

"Walk to your refrigerator," Margaret said.

Mary climbed down the steps, walked into the kitchen and opened her refrigerator. "Okay, it's open," she said.

"So, tell me. What's in there?" Margaret asked.

"Okay, there's milk, cheese, yogurt, strawberry jelly, some sticks of salami," Mary replied. "Applesauce, lunch meat, hot mustard, hot dogs…"

Margaret laughed. "Okay, you can stop," she said. "Where's the Diet Pepsi?"

"What?" Mary asked.

"Where's your Diet Pepsi?" Margaret repeated. "When I used to come and visit you, I could barely find room for anything because of all the Diet Pepsi."

"Well, we don't have room for them in the fridge anymore," Mary said with a shrug. "So I just put ice in a cup and drink them that way."

"Why don't you have room in your fridge?" Margaret asked.

"Well, because Bradley, Clarissa and I all need to put different things into it," Mary replied.

"And are you angry because your Pepsi is now in the pantry?"

Mary shook her head. "No, of course not."

"So, you've changed for the people you love," Margaret said. "It wasn't a big decision on your part. But it was a change, and you did it to meet their needs. You don't resent them. You didn't even notice, but you changed. That's how it works."

Mary stared at the inside of the refrigerator for a while. "It was just a natural evolution," Mary said slowly.

"Aye, the changes you make are because you're changing," Margaret said. "I know that sounds a little obvious."

"No. No, Ma, it's brilliant," Mary replied. "I don't have to worry about change. I just need to let it happen. And when it does, I'll be ready and happy."

"That's right," Margaret said. "And you'll know what's right, because you'll feel it in your heart."

Mikey kicked Mary, and she rubbed her stomach and felt the little foot. "I already love him," Mary said. "Can I love him even more?"

"Oh, darling, the love you have for that little man will be fierce," she said. "And there will be a bond between you that defies science. There is nothing like the love between a mother and her child."

"I'll never regret the changes?" she asked.

"Well, there will be moments," Margaret replied. "Mine were generally at three in the morning after several days of no sleep when you'll wonder why in the world you decided to become a mother. Then your baby will look up at you and smile. Or he'll chuckle, a deep belly laugh. Or he'll take your finger and wrap his hand around it. And your heart will break all over again, and you'll know that it's the greatest job and the hardest job in the world."

"It sounds magical," Mary said.

"It is, darling," she said. "And you will be a wonderful mother. So, have I swept your worries away for the day?"

Mary laughed. "Yes, you have," she said. "I'm lucky to have you for my mother."

"And I'm just as lucky to have you for my little girl," Margaret replied. "I love you, Mary."

"I love you too, Ma."

Chapter Fifty-five

Bradley parked the cruiser in the driveway and hurried across the lawn to the house. Apprehension was building in his gut. There were no lights shining out of the windows, and Mary had been home alone most of the day. She'd told him that she wasn't worried about Julie anymore, but Julie was unlike any ghost they'd encountered. And, he had to admit, he felt responsible because Julie was in their home because of him.

He took the stairs two at a time and dashed to the front door, his worry overwhelming his common sense. Grabbing hold of the doorknob, the threw the door open. "Mary!" he called immediately as he stepped inside. Then he froze.

"What the hell?" he asked softly.

The furniture in the living room had been pushed to the sides of the room, or removed altogether. A large mirror ball somehow hung from the ceiling, and a hundred strands of crepe paper draped from the center of the room to the edges, creating a tent-like feel to the room. The lights were low, and thousands of tiny reflections from the ball sparkled throughout the room.

"Hi," Mary said, coming up and kissing him. "Welcome to Prom Night."

He shook his head. "This is amazing."

"Your outfit is laying out in the bedroom," she said. "You need to hurry because you're one of the guests of honor."

"I don't have to guess who the other one is, do I?" he asked.

Mary shook her head. "No, and she should be showing up any moment."

Bradley followed his usual routine of taking off his jacket, securing his gun, and then he went upstairs to see what Mary had in store for him. He looked at the clothes on the bed and shook his head. "It could have been worse," he said looking at the charcoal grey, stovepipe slacks, the striped, polyester shirt and the letterman sweater.

He was dressed and coming down the stairs in a matter of minutes. Mary looked up at him and smiled. "You look very handsome," she said.

"I feel like a dork," he replied. "And these pants are like floods."

She shrugged. "That's how they wore them in those days," she said.

He gazed slowly around the room. It was really incredible. "You outdid yourself," he said. "It feels like a prom."

Smiling she nodded, "And we even have old records and a record player. Stanley never throws anything out."

He looked down at the letterman sweater. "Yeah, well, I guess neither do I," he said.

She shook her head. "No, this is part of your history," she said. "And I'm really glad you saved it. It could make the difference between pulling this whole thing off or not."

"Okay, what do you want me to do?" he asked.

"Bend down," she said.

He did as she requested and she ran her hand through his hair, messing it up a little. "There," she said. "Your hair was too perfect."

Still bent over, his face only inches from hers, he met her eyes, and she felt the familiar warmth flood steal through her body. "You really are one sexy man," she teased with a sigh.

Lifting his hand to her neck, he caressed her gently, rubbing the underside of her jaw with his thumb. "How soon will she be here?" he asked.

Mary sighed. "Too soon," she said regretfully, stepping back. "But you definitely owe me a raincheck on that."

He straightened up, but kept his eyes on hers. "Yes," he said. "Yes I do."

Feeling a shiver of anticipation, she wrapped her arms around herself and sighed. "If your dad was even half as sexy as you are," she said, "I can totally understand her obsession."

She stepped away from him and went into the middle of the room. Tiny lights sparkled over her as the mirrored ball slowly spun. "Julie," she called out. "Julie, it's time."

Julie appeared immediately, and her jaw dropped when she looked around the room. "I don't understand," she breathed.

Mary walked over to the turntable and put the needle on the record. Strains of *Unchained Melody* filled the room, and Julie gasped in delight. Bradley walked towards her and smiled. "I think this might be our dance," he said.

She blushed, looked down at the ground, and then back up at Bradley. "Are you sure you want to dance with me?" she asked.

He nodded and smiled. "More than anything," he said.

She glided into his arms, and he slowly moved around the living room to the music.

"This is how I always dreamt it would be," she sighed. "I'm so sorry I made you crash your car."

Bradley stumbled over his feet. "What?" he asked.

She smiled up at him. "You know, you were driving with the other lady," she said, a bright smile on her face. "I wanted to see you, so I stepped out into the middle of the road."

Her smile disappeared. "And then your car swerved off the road," she continued. "I'm so glad you didn't get hurt."

Bradley stepped back, away from her, shaking his head. "Someone did get hurt," he said. "My parents. My parents were in that car. My parents died in that car accident."

She shook her head. "No, it was you in the car," she insisted. "You were driving it. You turned the wheel because you thought I was real. It wasn't anyone else."

The song ended, and Bradley took a deep breath. "If you'll excuse me for a moment," he said.

She smiled. "And then we'll dance some more, right?"

He nodded, his mind a hundred miles away. "Sure, right."

Chapter Fifty-six

Bradley found Mary in the dining room, pulling the next record out of its sleeve. "How's it going in there?" she asked. Then she saw Bradley's face. She put the record on the table and hurried over to him. "Darling, what's wrong?"

"She…" he paused. He couldn't bring himself to say it.

"Yes?" Mary asked.

He looked back over his shoulder, and then he looked at Mary. "She killed my parents," he finally said.

Mary shook her head in shock. "How?" she replied, at a loss for words.

"She just apologized for causing my car to crash," he said. "She said she saw me driving with another woman, and she stepped out onto the road. The car swerved to avoid her and crashed."

The pain in his eyes was almost unbearable. She couldn't ask him to help her save the person who had destroyed his young life. "I'll call Mike," she said, placing her hand on his arm. "We don't have to help her. Someone else can do this."

His eyes widened, and he took a deep breath. "No," he said, his voice resolute. "No, I'm okay. No, actually, I'm better than okay. I have a feeling this is what my dad would want me to do."

She smiled at him and nodded. "I'm sure he would," she said.

He walked back into the living room, and Mary put on the next record, *My Girl,* then walked over to the living room to watch. Bradley smiled down at Julie and spoke with her as they danced. Julie's eyes were beaming with adoration as she danced with him. And they both clapped when the song was over. Mary had set up a record to drop down automatically and start playing. She really hadn't been paying too much attention when she'd put it on, and then the song *Strange Things Happen* started to play.

It was like watching a scene from a movie. As the song came on, Bradley shrugged off his letterman sweater and put it on Julie.

The lyrics from the song wafted through the room, a young man singing about a girl he met at a dance.

"That's like us," Julie said to Bradley. "We're both at a dance together."

He nodded. "Yes," he said. "Do you remember this song?"

298

She listened for a moment, and her smile dropped. "This is the dead girl song, isn't it?" she asked sadly. "She takes his sweater, and he finds it on her gravestone."

Bradley nodded. "Yes, you do remember it."

Her look of adoration turned into one of possessiveness. "I'm not like that girl," she said slowly. "I'm not going to give back the sweater."

Bradley felt a cold chill wash over him. "Julie, you wanted to go to prom," Bradley said. "That's what was keeping you on this side. You were supposed to go to prom with Blake."

She shook her head. "No, Blake never asked me to go to prom with him," she said, her smile widening. "No one ever asked me out because I was "Crazy Julie," and most people were afraid of me."

Bradley glanced over to Mary, and she nodded, her eyes as wide as saucers. She'd heard Julie's pronouncement. It hadn't been a broken heart or a missed dance that caused Julie's behavior. Julie had been disturbed before she died and had carried that trait with her after her death.

Mary stepped back into the dining room. "Mike," she whispered urgently. "I need some intervention here, and I really need it now."

She hurried back to the living room and saw Julie with her head on Bradley's chest, slowly

299

dancing to the song, humming to herself. He looked over to Mary and shook his head, uncertain of what he should do.

"I love dancing with you," Julie said. "I've dreamed about this for so many years. And now that you're here, we can dance together forever."

"Forever?" Bradley asked, his blood running cold. "What do you mean by that?"

She sighed happily. "Once the music stops, I'm going to take you with me," she replied. "Where we can be together for always."

Chapter Fifty-seven

Mary pulled out her phone, clicked on the radio app and accessed an oldies channel. She wasn't going to take any chances with the record player. She wanted non-stop music for now. She synced her phone with the Bluetooth speakers in the living room, and music streamed out of them. She slowly increased the volume, so her music came up as the record was finishing. The familiar strains of *Baby I'm Yours* filled the room, and Julie looked around.

"I love that song," she said, starting to sing along. "In other words, until the end of time."

Bradley shot a *Really?* look and Mary shook her head and shrugged. She had no control of the music at this point.

"Actually, Julie," Bradley said, "about the whole end of time thing…"

Julie looked up and smiled at him. "Oh, don't worry," she said. "I know that as a human you can't stay with me until the end of time."

Bradley was pretty sure he wasn't going to be happy with the rest of her thought. "So, I'm going to kill you," she continued happily.

"No. No you're not," Mary said, walking into the room.

Bradley looked at Mary and shook his head. "Get out of here," he said.

Julie turned and Mary saw all of the crazy in her eyes for the first time and held back a gasp. "I'm taking him with me," Julie said. "Then I'll go and never return."

Mary shook her head. "No, that's not an option," she said. "He stays, and you go. You got your dance. You got prom. Now you cross over."

Julie smiled at Mary and then turned her gaze back to Bradley. "It's time to go now," she sang.

Like a cold, steel vise, Bradley felt pressure around his neck, cutting off the air.

"Don't worry," Julie said. "It doesn't take very long."

Mary whipped her arms in Julie's direction, praying for residual effects, but nothing happened. And Bradley's face was turning purple.

"No!" she screamed, running at Julie. "No, you can't kill him."

Mary felt the cold, but she had no impact on the crazed spirit. "Please!" Mary screamed. "Someone help me."

"Julie." Bradley's voice came from behind Mary. She spun around and saw Bradley's spirit walking across the room.

"Oh, no," Mary cried, slowly dropping to her knees.

Bradley's human form dropped onto the ground while Julie turned toward the voice. She smiled at him. "That was fast," she said.

He nodded. "Are you ready to go with me?" he asked. "To cross over?"

She paused, looking skeptical. "If I cross over can I come back?" she asked.

He shook his head. "No, but we'll be together. Forever."

"Bradley, don't go," Mary cried. "Fight it. We both know you can fight it."

He smiled down at Mary. "I'll be a great guardian angel," he said.

"No," she sobbed, wrapping her arms around her stomach. "No, I can't do this without you."

He shook his head. "Don't worry," he said. "Things will be fine."

Then he held out his hand. "Come on Julie," he said. "Before Mary convinces me to stay."

Julie looked at Mary and then at the spirit in front of her and nodded. "Okay," she said with a casual shrug. "I'll go."

She took his hand and he led her forward. "Good-bye, Mary," he called and then they both faded away.

Chapter Fifty-eight

Mary stared in disbelief at the place in the room where they faded away. "No," she cried, shaking her head, sobs wracking her body. "No, this wasn't supposed to happen."

Then she heard a cough.

She turned. Her breath caught in her throat and she looked at Bradley's body on the ground. "Cough. Cough. Cough."

She crawled across the floor to him. He was breathing! His skin had color to it, and he was coughing. She threw herself into his arms. "Oh, Bradley," she sobbed. "You came back."

He wrapped his arms around her and held her. "I didn't leave," he whispered, his voice hoarse. "He came. He came before I was unconscious."

"Who came?" she asked. "I saw you. I saw you there."

"My dad," Bradley said. "I heard his voice in my head. He told me to drop." Bradley was crying, too. "My dad came back and saved me."

She wiped her tears with her palms and shook her head. "Okay, you can't die," she said. "You don't know what I just went through." She trembled and inhaled sharply. "I really thought I'd lost you."

He held her and kissed her. "No, I won't die," he promised her. "I'll always be here for you."

She lay in his arms for several minutes. Then she finally looked up at him. "Your dad? That was your dad?"

She could feel the rumble of his chuckle through his chest. He continued to hold her and nodded. "It was really strange," he said. "It was like he was in my head."

He turned and looked at her. "I didn't know you went to his gravesite," he said.

"Oh, well, I actually went to see Jeannine," she said. "But since he was there…"

He smiled at her. "You thought you'd give him a piece of your mind?" he asked.

"I was polite," she said, laying her head on his shoulder.

"He told me he was proud of me," Bradley said, awe in his voice. "He said that he'd always been proud of me but didn't know how to say it. And then…"

His voice broke. Mary lifted her head and met his eyes. "What did he say?"

"He said he'd been watching me and was proud of the man I'd become," he said softly.

She reached up and kissed him. "I like your dad," she said.

Bradley smiled. "I think he likes you, too," he said.

Just then Mikey kicked them both, and Bradley smiled at Mary. "I heard him tell you he was going to be a guardian angel," he said.

"Yeah, well, I'm feeling much better about that comment knowing that was your dad and not you," she said.

"Me too," he said, kissing her again. "Me, too."

Chapter Fifty-nine

Mary woke up Saturday morning and was surprised to see the sun shining through her window. She glanced at the clock to see that it was already past nine o'clock. "Good grief," she said, pushing her hair out of her face. "How in the world did I sleep so long?"

Pushing herself out of bed, she walked across the room and out into the hallway. "Bradley?" she called, still a little anxious from the night before.

"Good! You're up," he called from downstairs. "Don't come downstairs if you're not decent."

"My sister's always decent."

"Sean?" she asked.

"Aye, he's down here eating all the doughnuts."

"Ian?"

"Yeah, he's down here, too. Using his hypno-spells and trying to get the rest of us to do all the work."

"Rick?"

"Honey, why don't you get dressed, and then you can come down and see everyone in person?" Bradley laughed.

"Okay," she said. "I'll be down in a few minutes."

By the time she took a shower, got dressed and put on makeup, it was a little longer than a few minutes. But there was no way she was going downstairs to a group of good-looking men without looking her best. And, she thought, when she stepped off the stairs and saw the group of them dressed in t-shirts and jeans with tool belts slung low on their hips, the wait was worth it.

"Dang," she whispered.

"Mary," Ian was the first to see her. He hurried over and gave her a kiss. "You're looking gorgeous, darling. Would you care for a wee bit of breakfast?"

"What are you all doing here?" she asked.

"Well," Sean said, grabbing a chocolate-covered, Bavarian cream-filled long john from the doughnut box and bringing it over to her. "We're going to fix your kitchen today."

She looked at the group of smiling eager men and shook her head. "I really hate to ask," she said, "because I love you all for doing this, but does anyone here know what they're doing?"

"Don't worry, girlie," Stanley said, coming around the kitchen entrance in a pair of baggy overalls and a flannel shirt. "I'm in charge here."

"In charge of sitting around and chewing the fat," Ian teased.

Bradley came over and kissed her. "Don't worry," he said with a wink. "We've got this covered. The guys got here early, and we watched a video on youtube."

She laughed aloud. "Well, if you watched a video, you're pretty much experts," she said.

"Aye, and next we'll be rewiring the house," Ian teased.

She looked around for a moment.

"What are you looking for?" Bradley asked.

"Um, Mike," she said. "I'm hoping he still has contacts with the fire department."

"Sweetheart, don't worry," Bradley said. "What could go wrong?"

She looked at him and felt a surge of love flow through her. This man, this wonderful man, was her partner in every sense of the word. And she knew, he would never, ever let her down.

"Nothing," she said to him, love shining in her eyes. "Nothing could go wrong."

"Do you want to watch?" Sean asked as he pressed the electric screwdriver to make it rev up.

She grinned. "Maybe I'll go to the store and get things for lunch."

Bradley kissed her again. "Great idea," he said. "Thanks."

"Okay, you whippersnappers," Stanley called. "Let me show you how a real man uses power tools."

Mary giggled and shook her head. "I better get out of here before the testosterone affects the baby," she said.

Bradley helped her stand up. "I love you, Mary Alden," he said.

"And I love you, Bradley Alden," she replied.

Chapter Sixty

Snow was falling, a light dusting that turned the empty farmers' fields into a winter wonderland. Mary turned off Highway 20 onto Browns Mill Road. She drove past the entrance to the Stephenson County Convention and Visitors Bureau building, with a parking lot filled with people traveling to Galena for the Thanksgiving weekend, and continued a little farther up the street.

The new SUV they bought several weeks ago was four-wheel drive and handled well on the gravel road she pulled into, and the snowy ground didn't affect the traction at all. Mary parked off the road and slipped her gloves on before she climbed out of the vehicle.

The stone marker next to the drive had "Gund Cemetery, Established 1850" carved into its face. Mary walked past the marker and underneath the ornate, wrought iron archway into the long and narrow strip of hallowed ground.

She'd been coming here for the past few weeks, once she had learned the history from a friend in German Valley. In the late 1800s a town had been established a little north of where the cemetery stood. But when the cholera epidemic struck, the entire town had been hit hard — so much so that all the survivors could manage was a large, mass grave in the center of the cemetery, the sole marker being an ancient oak tree.

During Mary's first visit, several small children had come over to talk to her. They were open and trusting, and she had no problem teaching them how to look for and walk into the light. But now, most of the children were gone, and she was working with the adults. It was a slow process, but she felt that she was beginning to gain their trust.

She walked over to the oak tree, its leaves brown and leathery, still attached to the branches. As soon as she got within the canopy of the oak, the spirits began to appear.

"Good morning," Mary said to one of the women she'd seen before.

This time the woman approached her. "I need to show you something," she said, motioning urgently to Mary.

Mary followed, interested to see what the woman wanted to show her. They walked to the edge of the cemetery, and the woman pointed out into the distance. "Do you see her?" she asked, her arm raised. "There in the field?"

Mary squinted her eyes, and sure enough, the air seemed to vibrate and then solidify. She could see the spirit of a young woman standing in the field, looking around. The spirit glided around the area, as if she was searching for something, and then turned and looked the other way.

"She's not one of us," the spirit standing next to Mary said. "She's only been out there for a little while. And I think she's lost."

Pulling her cell phone out of her purse, Mary dialed Bradley's number. "Hi, it's me," she said when he answered. "I think you need to come out and meet me at Gund Cemetery. I have a feeling I may have just stumbled upon a homicide victim."

# # #

About the author: Terri Reid lives near Freeport, the home of the Mary O'Reilly Mystery Series, and loves a good ghost story. She loves hearing from her readers at author@terrireid.com

Other Books by Terri Reid:

Mary O'Reilly Paranormal Mystery Series:

Mary O'Reilly Short Stories

316

Made in the USA
Monee, IL
18 June 2021

71692498R00177